Love at
Second Sight

Love at
Second Sight
Ada Leverson

MINT EDITIONS

Love at Second Sight was first published in 1916.

This edition published by Mint Editions 2021.

ISBN 9781513283173 | E-ISBN 9781513288192

Published by Mint Editions®

 MINT
EDITIONS

minteditionbooks.com

Publishing Director: Jennifer Newens
Design & Production: Rachel Lopez Metzger
Project Manager: Micaela Clark
Typesetting: Westchester Publishing Services

Contents

I

An appalling crash, piercing shrieks, a loud, unequal quarrel on a staircase, the sharp bang of a door. . .

Edith started up from her restful corner on the blue sofa by the fire, where she had been thinking about her guest, and rushed to the door.

"Archie—Archie! Come here directly! What's that noise?"

A boy of ten came calmly into the room.

"It wasn't me that made the noise," he said, "it was Madame Frabelle."

His mother looked at him. He was a handsome, fair boy with clear grey eyes that looked you straight in the face without telling you anything at all, long eyelashes that softened, but gave a sly humour to his glance, a round face, a very large forehead, and smooth straw-coloured hair. Already at this early age he had the expressionless reserve of the public school where he was to be sent, with something of the suave superiority of the university for which he was intended. Edith thought he inherited both of these traits from her.

She gazed at him, wondering, as she had often wondered, at the impossibility of guessing, even vaguely, what was really going on behind that large brow. And he looked back observantly, but not expressively, at her. She was a slim, fair, pretty woman, with more vividness and character than usually goes with her type. Like the boy, she had long-lashed grey eyes, and *blond-cendre* hair: her mouth and chin were of the Burne-Jones order, and her charm, which was great but unintentional, and generally unconscious, appealed partly to the senses and partly to the intellect. She was essentially not one of those women who irritate all their own sex by their power (and still more by their fixed determination) to attract men; she was really and unusually indifferent to general admiration. Still, that she was not a cold woman, not incapable of passionate feeling, was obvious to any physiognomist; the fully curved lips showed her generous and pleasure-loving temperament, while the softly glancing, intelligent, smiling eyes spoke fastidiousness and discrimination. Her voice was low and soft, with a vibrating sound in it, and she laughed often and easily, being very ready to see and enjoy the amusing side of life. But observation and emotion alike were instinctively veiled by a quiet, reposeful manner, so that she made herself further popular by appearing retiring. Edith Ottley might so easily have been the centre of any group, and yet—she was not! Women were grateful to her, and in return admitted that she was pretty, unaffected and charming. Today she was dressed very simply in dark blue and might have passed for Archie's elder sister.

"It isn't anything. It wasn't my fault. It was her fault. Madame Frabelle said *she* would teach me to take away her mandolin and use it for a cricket bat. She needn't teach me; I know already."

"Now, Archie, you know perfectly well you've no right to go into her room when she isn't there."

"How can I go in when she is there? . . . She won't let me. Besides, I don't want to."

"It isn't nice of you; you ought not to go into her room without her permission."

"It isn't her room; it's your room. At least, it's the spare room."

"Have you done any harm to the mandolin?"

He paused a little, as he often did before answering, as if in absence of mind, and then said, as though starting up from a reverie:

"Er—no. No harm."

"Well, what have you done?"

"I can mend it," he answered.

"Madame Frabelle has been very kind to you, Archie. I'm sorry you're not behaving nicely to a guest in your mother's house. It isn't the act of a gentleman."

"Oh. Well, there are a great many things in her room, Mother; some of them are rather jolly."

"Go and say you're sorry, Archie. And you mustn't do it again."

"Will it be the act of a gentleman to say I'm sorry? It'll be the act of a story-teller, you know."

"What! Aren't you sorry to have bothered her?"

"I'm sorry she found it out," he said, as he turned to the door.

"These perpetual scenes and quarrels between my son and my guest are most painful to me," Edith said, with assumed solemnity.

He looked grave. "Well, she needn't have quarrelled."

"But isn't she very kind to you?"

"Yes, she isn't bad sometimes. I like it when she tells me lies about what her husband used to do—I mean stories. She's not a bad sort. . . Is she a homeless refugette, Mother?"

"Not exactly that. She's a widow, and she's staying with us, and we must be nice to her. Now, you won't forget again, will you?"

"Right. But I can mend it."

"I think I'd better go up and see her," said Edith.

Archie politely opened the door for his mother.

"I shouldn't, if I were you," he said.

Edith slowly went back to the fire.

"Well, I'll leave her a little while, perhaps. Now do go and do something useful."

"What, useful? Gracious! I haven't got much more of my holidays, Mother."

"That's no reason why you should spend your time in worrying everybody, and smashing the musical instruments of guests that are under your roof."

He looked up at the ceiling and smiled, as if pleased at this way of putting it.

"I suppose she's very glad to have a roof to her mouth—I mean to her head," he hurriedly corrected. "But, Mother, she isn't poor. She has an amber necklace. Besides, she gave Dilly sixpence the other day for not being frightened of a cow. If she can afford to give a little girl sixpence for every animal she says she isn't afraid of!" . . .

"That only proves she's kind. And I didn't say she was poor; that's not the point. We must be nice and considerate to anyone staying with us—don't you see?"

He became absent-minded again for a minute.

"Well, I shouldn't be surprised if she'll be able to use it again," he said consolingly—"the mandolin, I mean. Besides, what's the good of it anyway? I say, Mother, are all foreigners bad-tempered?"

"Madame Frabelle is not a foreigner."

"I never said she was. But her husband was. He used to get into frightful rages with her sometimes. She says he was a noble fellow. She liked him awfully, but she says he never understood her. Do you suppose she talked English to him?"

"That's enough, Archie. Go and find something to do."

As he went out he turned round again and said:

"Does father like her?"

"Why, yes, of course he does."

"How funny!" said Archie. "Well, I'll say I'm sorry. . . when I see her again."

Edith kissed him, a proceeding that he bore heroically. He was kissable, but she seldom gave way to the temptation. Then she went back to the sofa. She wanted to go on thinking about that mystery, her guest.

II

M adame Frabelle had arrived about a fortnight ago, with a letter of introduction from Lady Conroy. Lady Conroy herself was a vague, amiable Irishwoman, with a very large family of children. She and Edith, who knew each other slightly before, had grown intimate when they met, the previous summer, at a French watering-place. The letter asked Edith, with urgent inconsequence, to be kind to Madame Frabelle, of whom Lady Conroy said nothing except that she was of good family—she had been a Miss Eglantine Pollard—and was the widow of a well-to-do French wine merchant.

She was described as a clever, interesting woman who wished to study English life in her native land. It did not surprise Lady Conroy in the least that an Englishwoman should wish to study English in England; but she was a woman who was never surprised at anything except the obvious and the inevitable.

Edith had not had the faintest idea of asking Madame Frabelle to stay at her very small house in Sloane Street, for which invitation, indeed, there seemed no possible need or occasion. Yet she found herself asking her visitor to stay for a few days until a house or a hotel should be found; and Bruce, who detested guests in the house, seconded the invitation with warmth and enthusiasm. As Bruce was a subconscious snob, he may have been slightly influenced by the letter from Lady Conroy, who was the wife of an unprominent Cabinet Minister and, in a casual way, rather *grande dame*, if not exactly smart. But this consideration could not weigh with Edith, and its effect on Bruce must have long passed away. Madame Frabelle accepted the invitation as a matter of course, made use of it as a matter of convenience, and had remained ever since, showing no sign of leaving. Edith was deeply interested in her.

AND BRUCE WAS MORE GENUINELY impressed and unconsciously bored by Madame Frabelle than by any woman he had ever met. Yet she was not at all extraordinary. She was a tall woman of about fifty, well bred without being distinguished, who could never have been handsome but was graceful, dignified, and pleasing. She was neither dark nor fair. She had a broad, good-natured face, and a pale, clear complexion. She was inclined to be fat; not locally, in the manner of a pincushion, but with the generally diffused plumpness described in shops as stock size.

She was not the sort of modern woman of fifty, with a thin figure and a good deal of rouge, who looks young from the back when dancing or walking, and talks volubly and confidentially of her young men. She had, of course, nothing of the middle-aged woman of the past, who at her age would have been definitely on the shelf, doing wool-work or collecting recipes there. Nor did she resemble the strong-minded type in perpetual tailor-made clothes, with short grey hair and eye-glasses, who belongs to clubs and talks chiefly of the franchise. Madame Frabelle was soft, womanly, amiable, yet extremely outspoken, very firm, and inclined to lay down the law. She was certainly charming, as Bruce and Edith agreed every day (even now, when they were beginning to wonder when she was going away!). She had an extraordinary amount of personal magnetism, since she convinced both the Ottleys, as she had convinced Lady Conroy, that she was wonderfully clever: in fact, that she knew everything.

A fortnight had passed, and Edith was beginning to grow doubtful. Was she so clever? Did she know everything? Did she know anything at all? Long arguments, that grew quite heated and excited at luncheon or dinner, about the origin of a word, the author of a book, and various debatable questions of the kind, invariably ended, after reference to a dictionary or an encyclopaedia, in Madame Frabelle proving herself, with an air of triumph, to be completely and entirely wrong. She was as generally positive as she was fatally mistaken. Yet so intense a belief had she in her intuition as well as in her own inaccurate information that her hypnotised hosts were growing daily more and more under her thumb. She took it for granted that everyone would take her for granted—and everyone did.

Was all this agreeable or otherwise? Edith thought it must be, or how could they bear it at all? If it had not been extremely pleasant it would have been simply impossible.

The fair, gentle, pretty Edith, who was more subtle than she appeared on the surface, while apparently indolent, had a very active brain. Madame Frabelle caused her to use it more than she had ever done before. Edith was intensely curious and until she understood her visitor she could not rest satisfied. She made her a psychological study.

For example, here was a curious little point. Madame Frabelle did not look young for her age, nor did she seem in the least inclined to wish to be admired, nor ever to have been a flirt. The word "fast", for example, would have been quite grotesque as associated with her, though she was by no means prudish as to subjects of conversation, nor prim in the middle-class way. Yet somehow it would not have seemed incongruous or surprising if one had found out that there was even now some romance in her life. But, doubtless, the most striking thing about her—and what made her popular—was her intense interest in other people. It went so far as to reach the very verge of being interference; but she was so pleasant that one could scarcely resent it either as curiosity or intrusion. Since she had stayed with the Ottleys, she appeared to think of no-one and nothing else in the world. One would think that no-one else existed for her. And, after all, such extreme interest is flattering. Bruce, Archie, Edith, even Dilly's nurse, all had, in her, an audience: interested, absorbed, enchanted. Who could help enjoying it?

EDITH WAS STILL THINKING ABOUT Madame Frabelle when a few minutes later, Bruce came in.

Bruce also was fair, besides being tall, good-looking and well built. Known by their friends for some reason as the little Ottleys, these two were a rather fine-looking pair, and (at a casual glance) admirably suited to one another. They appeared to be exactly like thousands of other English married couples of the upper middle class between thirty and forty; he looked as manly (through being sunburnt from knocking a little ball over the links) as if he habitually went tiger-shooting; but, though not without charm, he had much less distinction than his wife. Most people smiled when Bruce's name was mentioned, and it was usual for his intimates to clap him on the back and call him a silly ass, which proves he was not unpopular. On the other hand, Edith was described as a very pretty woman, or a nice little thing, and by the more discriminating, jolly clever when you know her, and don't you forget it.

When Bruce told his wife that no-one had ever regretted consulting him on a difficult, secret, and delicate matter, Edith had said she was quite sure they hadn't. Perhaps she thought no-one had ever regretted consulting him on such a subject, simply because no-one had ever tried.

"Oh, please don't move, Edith," he said, in the tone which means, "Oh, please do move." "I like to see you comfortable."

There was something in his manner that made her feel apologetic, and she changed her position with the feeling of guilt about nothing, and a tinge of shame for something she hadn't done, easily produced by an air of self-sacrifice Bruce was apt to show at such moments.

"Your hair's coming down, Edith," he said kindly, to add to her vague embarrassment.

As a matter of fact, a curl by the right ear was only about one-tenth of an inch farther on the cheek than it was intended to be But, by this observation, he got the advantage of her by giving the impression that she looked wild, unkempt, and ruffled, though she was, in reality, exactly as trim and neat as always.

"Well—about the delicate matter you were going to talk over with me, Bruce?"

"Oh yes. Oh, by the way," he said, "before we go into that, I wonder if you could help me about something? You could do me a really great service by helping me to find a certain book."

"Why, of course, Bruce, with pleasure. What is the book?" asked the amiable wife, looking alert.

Bruce looked at her with pity.

"What is the book? My dear Edith, don't you see I shouldn't have come to you about it if I knew what the book was."

"I beg your pardon, Bruce," said Edith, now feeling thoroughly in the wrong, and looking round the room. "But if you can't give me the name of the book I scarcely see how I can find it."

"And if I knew its name I shouldn't want your assistance."

It seemed a deadlock.

Going to the bookcase, Edith said:

"Can't you give me some idea of what it's like?"

"Certainly I can. I've seen it a hundred times in this very room; in fact it's always here, except when it's wanted."

Edith went down on her knees in front of the bookcase and cross-questioned Bruce on the physiognomy of the volume. She asked whether it was a novel, whether it was blue, whether it belonged to the library, whether it was Stevenson, whether it was French, or if it was suitable for the children.

To all of these questions he returned a negative.

"Suitable for the children?" he repeated. "What a fantastic idea! Do you think I should take all this trouble to come and request your assistance and spend hours of valuable time looking for a book that's suitable for the children?"

"But, Bruce, if you request my assistance without having the slightest idea of what book it is, how shall I possibly be able to help?"

"Quite so. . . . quite so. Never mind, Edith, don't trouble. If I say that it's a pity there isn't more order in the house you won't regard it, I hope, dear, as a reproach in any way. If there were a place for everything, and everything in its place—However! Never mind. It's a small matter, and it can't be helped. I know, Edith dear, you were not brought up to be strictly orderly. Some people are not. I don't blame you; not in the least. Still, when Dilly grows up I shall be sorry if—"

"Bruce, it's nothing to do with order. The room is perfectly tidy. It's a question of your memory. You don't remember the name of the book."

"Pardon me, it's not a question of remembering the name; that would be nothing. Anyone can forget a name. That wouldn't matter."

"Oh, then, you mean you don't even know in the least what you want?"

At this moment Bruce decided it was time to find the book, and suddenly sprang, like a middle-aged fawn, at the writing-table, seizing a volume triumphantly.

"There it is—the whole time!" he said, "staring at you while you are helplessly looking for it. Oh, Edith, Edith!" he laughed amiably. "How like a woman that is! And the very book a few inches from your hand! Well, well, never mind; it's found at last. I hope, dear, in the future you will be more careful. We'll say no more about it now."

Edith didn't point out to Bruce that the book was a novel; that it was blue; that it belonged to the library, was French, and that it was still suitable for the children.

"Well, well," he said, sitting down with the book, which he had never wanted at all, and had never even thought of when he came to the room first, "well, well, here it is! And now for the point I was going to tell you when I came in."

"Shall we have tea, dear?" said Edith.

"Tea? Oh, surely not. It's only just four. I don't think it's good for the servants having tea half-an-hour earlier than usual. It's a little thing—yes, I know that, but I don't believe in it. I like punctuality, regularity—oh, well, of course, dear, if you wish it."

"No, I don't at all! I thought you might."

"Oh no. I like punctuality, er—and, as a matter of fact, I had tea at the club."

Laughing, Edith rang the bell.

Bruce lighted a cigarette, first, with his usual courtesy, asking her permission.

"I'll tell you about *that* when Woodhouse has gone," he said mysteriously.

"Oh, can't you tell me anything about it now? I wouldn't have ordered tea if I'd known that!"

He enjoyed keeping her waiting, and was delighted at her interest. He would have made it last longer, but was unable to bear his own suspense; so he said:

"Before I say any more, tell me: where is Madame Frabelle?"

III

"Madame Frabelle's in her own room. She stays there a good deal, you know. I fancy she does it out of tactfulness." Edith spoke thoughtfully.

"What does she do there?" Bruce asked with low-toned curiosity, as he stood up and looked in the glass.

"She says she goes there to read. She thinks it bores people to see a visitor sitting reading about the house; she says it makes them get tired of the sight of her."

"But she can't be reading all those hours, surely?" and Bruce sat down, satisfied with his appearance.

"One would think not. I used to think she was probably lying on the sofa with cold cream on her face, or something of that sort. But she doesn't. Once I went in," Edith smiled, "and found her doing Swedish exercises."

"Good heavens! What a wonderful woman she is! Do you mean to say she's learning Swedish, as well as all the other languages she knows?"

"No, no. I mean physical exercises. But go on, Bruce. I'm getting so impatient."

Bruce settled himself down comfortably, blew a ring of smoke, and then began slowly:

"I never dreamt, Edith—"

"Oh, Bruce, are you going to tell me everything you never dreamt? We shall take weeks getting to the point."

"Don't be absurd. I'll get to the point at once then. Look here; I think we ought to give a dinner for Madame Frabelle!"

"Oh, is that all? Of course! I've been wondering that you didn't wish to do it long before now."

"Have you? I'll tell you why. Thinking Madame Frabelle was a pal, er—a friend—of the Conroys, it stood to reason, don't you see, that she knew everyone in London; or could, if she liked—everyone worth knowing, I mean. Under these circumstances there was no point in—well—in showing off our friends to her. But I found out, only last night"—he lowered his voice—"what do you think? She isn't an intimate friend of Lady Conroy's at all! She only made her acquaintance in the drawing-room of the Royal Hotel two days before she came to London!"

Edith laughed.

"How delightful! Then why on earth did Lady Conroy send her to us with a letter of introduction? Why just us?"

"Because she likes you. Besides, it's just like her, isn't it? And she never said she had known her all her life. We jumped to that conclusion. It was our own idea."

"And how did you find it out?"

"Why, when you went up to the children and left me alone with Madame Frabelle yesterday evening, she told me herself; perfectly frankly, in her usual way. She's always like that, so frank and open. Besides, she hadn't the slightest idea we didn't know it."

"I hope you didn't let her think—" Edith began.

"Edith! As if I would! Well, that being so"—he lit another cigarette—"and under the circumstances, I want to ask some people to meet her. See?"

"She seems very happy with us alone, doesn't she? Not as if she cared much for going out."

"Yes, I know; that's all very well. But I don't want her to think we don't know anyone. And it seems a bit selfish, too, keeping her all to ourselves like this."

"Who do you want her to meet, dear?"

"I want her to meet the Mitchells," said Bruce. "It's only a chance, of course, that she hasn't met them already here, and I've told Mitchell at the Foreign Office a good deal about her. He's very keen to know her. Very keen indeed," he added thoughtfully.

"And then the Mitchells will ask her to their house, of course?"

"I know they will," said Bruce, rather jealously. "Well, I shan't mind her going there—once or twice—it's a very pleasant house, you know, Edith. And she likes celebrities, and clever people, and that sort of thing."

"Mrs. Mitchell will count her as one, no doubt."

"I daresay! What does that matter? So she is."

"I know she is, in a way; but, Bruce, don't you wonder why she stays here so long? I mean, there's no question of its not being for—well, for, say, interested reasons. I happen to know for a fact that she has a far larger income for herself alone than we have altogether. She showed me her bank-book one day."

"Why?"

"I don't know. She's so confidential, and perhaps she wanted me to know how she was placed. And—she's not that sort of person—she's generous and liberal, rather extravagant I should say."

"Quite so. Still, it's comfortable here, and saves trouble—and she likes us."

Bruce again looked up toward the mirror, though he couldn't see it now.

"Well, I don't mind her being here; it's a nice change, but it seems odd she hasn't said a word about going. Well, about the dinner. Who else shall we have, Edith? Let it be a small, intimate, distinguished sort of dinner. She hates stiffness and ceremony. She likes to have a chance to talk."

"She does, indeed. All right, you can leave it to me, Bruce. I'll make it all right. We'll have about eight people, shall we?"

"She must sit next to me, on my left," Bruce observed. "And not lilies of the valley—she doesn't like the scent."

Madame Frabelle was usually designated between them by the personal pronoun only.

"All right. But what was the delicate, difficult matter that someone consulted you about, Bruce?"

"Ah, I was just coining to that. . . Hush!"

The door opened. Madame Frabelle came in, dressed in a violet tea-gown.

"Tea?" said Edith, holding out a cup.

"Yes, indeed! I'm always ready for tea, and you have such delightful tea, Edith dear!" (They had already reached the point of Christian names, though Edith always found Eglantine a little difficult to say.) "It's nice to see you back so early, Mr. Ottley."

"Wouldn't you like a slice of lemon?" said Bruce.

To offer her a slice of lemon with tea was, from Bruce, a tribute to the lady's talents.

"Oh no! Cream and sugar, please."

Madame Frabelle was looking very pleasant and very much at her ease as she sat down comfortably, taking the largest chair.

"I'm afraid that Archie has been bothering you today," Edith said, as she poured out tea.

"What!" exclaimed Bruce, with a start of horror.

"Oh no, no, no! Not the least in the world, Mr. Ottley! He's a most delightful boy. We were only having some fun together—about my mandolin; that was all!"

(Edith thought of the sounds she had heard on the stairs.)

"I'm afraid I got a little cross. A thing I very seldom do." Madame Frabelle looked apologetically at Edith. "But we've quite made it up now! Oh, and by the way, I want to speak to you both rather seriously about your boy," she went on earnestly. She had a rather powerful, clear, penetrating voice, and spoke with authority, decision, and the sort of voluble fluency generally known as not letting anyone else get a word in edgeways.

"About our boy?" said Bruce, handing the toast to her invitingly, while Edith put a cushion behind her back, for which Madame Frabelle gave a little gracious smile.

"About your boy. Do you know, I have a very curious gift, Mr. Ottley. I can always see in children what they're going to make a success of in life. Without boasting, I know you, Edith, are kind enough to believe that I'm an extraordinary judge of character. Oh, I've always been like that. I can't help it. I'll tell you now what you must make of your boy," she pursued. "He is a born musician!"

"A musician!" exclaimed both his parents at once, in great astonishment.

Madame Frabelle nodded. "That boy is a born composer! He has genius for music. Look at his broad forehead! Those grey eyes, so wide apart! I know, just at first one thinks too much from the worldly point of view of the success of one's son in life. But why go against nature? The boy's a genius!"

"But," ventured Edith, "Archie hasn't the slightest ear for music!"

"He dislikes music intensely," said Bruce. "Simply loathes it."

"He cried so much over his piano lessons that we were obliged to let him give them up. It used to make him quite ill—and his music mistress too," Edith said. "I remember she left the last time in hysterics."

"Yes, by Jove, I remember too. Pretty girl she was. She had a nervous breakdown afterwards," said Bruce rather proudly.

"No, dear; you're thinking of the other one—the woman who began to teach him the violin."

"Oh, am I?"

Madame Frabelle nodded her head with a smile.

"Nothing on earth to do with it, my dear! The boy's a born composer all the same. With that face he must be a musician!"

"Really! Funny he hates it so," said Bruce thoughtfully. "But still, I have no doubt—"

"Believe me, you can't go by his not liking his lessons," assured Madame Frabelle, as she ate a muffin. "That has nothing to do with it at all. The young Mozart—"

"Mozart? I thought he played the piano when he was only three?"

"Handel, I mean—or was it Meyerbeer? At any rate you'll see I'm right."

"You really think we ought to force him against his will to study music seriously, with the idea of his being a composer when he grows up, though he detests it?" asked his mother.

Madame Frabelle turned to Edith.

"Won't you feel proud when you see your son conducting his own opera, to the applause of thousands? Won't it be something to be the mother of the greatest English composer of the twentieth century?"

"It would be rather fun."

"We shan't hear quite so much about Strauss, Elgar, Debussy and all those people when Archie Ottley grows up," declared Madame Frabelle.

"I hear very little about them now," said Bruce.

"Well, how should you at the Foreign Office, or the golf-links, or the club?" asked Edith.

Bruce ignored Edith, and went on: "Perhaps he'll turn out to be a Lionel Monckton or a Paul Rubens. Perhaps he'll write comic opera revues or musical comedies."

"Oh dear, no," said their guest, shaking her head decidedly. "It will be the very highest class, the top of the tree! The real thing!"

"Madame Frabelle *may* be right, you know," said Bruce.

She leant back, smiling.

"I *know* I'm right! There's simply no question about it."

"Well, what do you think we ought to do about it?" said Edith. "He goes to a preparatory school now where they don't have any music lessons at all."

"All the better," she answered. "The sort of lessons he would get at a school would be no use to him."

"So I should think," murmured Edith.

"Leave it, say, for the moment, and when he comes back for his next holidays put him under a good teacher—a really great man. And you'll see!"

"I daresay we shall," said Bruce, considerably relieved at the postponement. "Funny though, isn't it, his not knowing one tune from another, when he's a born musician?"

It flashed across Edith what an immense bond of sympathy it was between Bruce and Madame Frabelle that neither of them was burdened with the slightest sense of humour.

When he presently went out (each of them preferred talking to Her alone, and She also enjoyed a *tête-à-tête* most) Madame Frabelle drew up her chair nearer to Edith and said:

"My dear, I'm going to tell you something. Don't be angry with me, or think me impertinent, but you've been very kind to me, and I look upon you as a real friend."

"It's very sweet of you," said Edith, feeling hypnotised, and as if she would gladly devote her life to Madame Frabelle.

"Well, I can see something. You are not quite happy."

"Not happy!" exclaimed Edith.

"No. You have a trouble, and I'd give anything to take it away."

Madame Frabelle looked at her with sympathy, pressed her hand, then looked away.

Edith knew she was looking away out of delicacy. Delicacy about what? It was an effort not to laugh; but, oddly enough, it was also an effort not to feel secretly miserable. She wondered, though, what she was unhappy about. She need not have troubled, for Madame Frabelle was quite willing to tell her. She was, indeed, willing to tell anyone anything. Perhaps that was the secret of her charm.

IV

It was utterly impossible, literally out of the question, that Madame Frabelle could know anything about the one trouble, the one danger, that so narrowly escaped being almost a tragedy, in Edith's life.

It was three years since Bruce, always inclined to vague, mild flirtations, had been positively carried off his feet, and literally taken away by a determined young art student, with red hair, who had failed to marry a friend of his. While Edith, with the children, was passing the summer holidays at Westgate, Bruce had sent her the strangest of letters, informing her that he and Mavis Argles could not live without one another, and had gone to Australia together, and imploring her to divorce him. The complication was increased by the fact that at that particular moment the most charming man Edith had ever met, Aylmer Ross, that eloquent and brilliant barrister, had fallen in love with her, and she had become considerably attracted to him. Her pride had been hurt at Bruce's conduct, but she had certainly felt it less bitterly, in one way, because she was herself so much fascinated by Aylmer and his devotion.

But Edith had behaved with cool courage and real unselfishness. She felt certain that Brace's mania would not last, and that if it did he would be miserable. Strangely, then, she had declined to divorce him, and waited. Her prophecy turned out correct, and by the time they arrived at their journey's end the red-haired lady was engaged to a commercial traveller whom she met on the boat. By then Bruce and she were equally convinced that in going to Australia they had decidedly gone too far.

So Brace came back, and Edith forgave him. She made one condition only (which was also her one revenge), that he should never speak about it, never mention the subject again.

Aylmer Ross, who had taken his romance seriously to heart, refused to be kept as *l'ami de la maison,* and as a platonic admirer. Deeply disappointed—for he was prepared to give his life to Edith and her children (he was a widower of independent means)—he had left England; she had never seen him since.

All this had been a real event, a real break in Edith's life. For the first few months after she suffered, missing the excitement of Aylmer's controlled passion, and his congenial society. Gradually she made herself—not forget it—but put aside, ignore the whole incident. It gave her genuine satisfaction to know that she had made a sacrifice for Bruce's sake. She was aware that he could not exist really satisfactorily without her, though perhaps he didn't know it. He needed her. At first she had endeavoured to remain separated from him, while apparently living together, from who knows what feeling of romantic fidelity to Aylmer, or pique at the slight shown her by her husband. Then she found that impossible. It would make him more liable to other complications and the whole situation too full of general difficulties. So now, for the last three years, they had been on much the same terms as they were before. Bruce had become, perhaps, less patronising, more respectful to her, and she a shade more gentle and considerate to him, as to a child. For she was generous and did not forgive by halves. There were moments of nervous irritation, of course, and of sentimental regret. On the whole, though, Edith was glad she had acted as she did. But if occasionally she felt her life a little dull and flat, if she missed some of the excitement of that eventful year, it was impossible for anyone to see it by her manner.

What could Madame Frabelle possibly know about it? What did that lady really suppose was the matter?

"WHAT DO YOU THINK I'M unhappy about?" Edith repeated.

Madame Frabelle, as has been mentioned, was willing to tell her. She told her, as usual, with fluency and inaccuracy.

Edith was much amused to find how strangely mistaken was this authoritative lady as to her intuitions, how inevitably à faux with her penetrations and her instinctive guesses. Madame Frabelle said that she believed Edith was beginning to feel the dawn of love for someone, and was struggling against it. (The struggle of course in reality had long been over.)

Who was the person?

"I haven't met him yet," Madame Frabelle said; "but isn't there a name I hear very often? Your husband is always talking about him; he told me I was to make the acquaintance of this great friend of his. Something tells me it is he. I shall know as soon as I see him. You can't hide it from me!"

Who was the person Bruce was always mentioning to Madame Frabelle? Certainly not Aylmer Ross—he had apparently forgotten his existence.

"Are you referring to—?"

Madame Frabelle looked out of the window and nodded.

"Yes—Mr. Mitchell!"

Edith started, and a smile curved her lips.

"It's always the husband's great friend, unfortunately," sighed Eglantine. "Oh, my dear" (with the usual cheap, ready-made knowingness of the cynic), "I've seen so much of that. Now I'm going to help you. I'm determined to leave you two dear, charming people without a cloud, when I go."

"You're not thinking of going?"

"Not yet. . . no. Not while you let me stay here, dear. I've friends in London, and in the country, but I haven't looked them up, or written to them, or done anything since I've been here. I've been too happy. I couldn't be bothered. I am so interested in you! Another thing—may I say?—for I feel as if I'd known you for years. You think your husband doesn't know it. You are wrong."

"Am I really?"

"Quite. Last night a certain look when he spoke of the Mitchells showed me that Bruce is terribly jealous. He doesn't show it, but he is."

"But—Mrs. Mitchell?" suggested Edith. "She's one of our best friends—a dear thing. By the way, we're asking them to dine with us on Tuesday."

"I'm delighted to hear it. I shall understand everything then. Isn't it curious—without even seeing them—that I know all about it? I think I've a touch of second sight."

"But, Eglantine, aren't you going a little far? Hadn't you better wait until you've seen them, at least. You've no idea how well the Mitchells get on."

"I've no doubt of it," she replied, "and, of course, I don't know that he—Mr. Mitchell, I mean—even realises what you are to him. But *I* do!"

Edith was really impressed at the dash with which Madame Frabelle so broadly handled this vague theme.

"Wait till you do see them," she said, rather mischievously, declining to deny her friend's suggestion altogether.

"Odd I should have guessed it, isn't it?" Madame Frabelle was evidently pleased. "You'll admit this, Edith, from what your husband says I gather you see each other continually, don't you?"

"Very often."

"Bruce and he are together at the Foreign Office. Bruce thinks much of him, and admires him. With it all I notice now and then a tinge of bitterness in the way he speaks. He was describing their fancy-dress ball to me the other day, and really his description of Mr. Mitchell's costume would have been almost spiteful in any other man."

"Well, but Mr. Mitchell is over sixty. And he was got up as a black poodle."

"Yes; quite so. But he's a fine-looking man, isn't he? And very pleasant and hospitable?"

"Oh yes, of course."

"On your birthday last week that magnificent basket of flowers came from Mr. Mitchell," stated Eglantine.

"Certainly; from the Mitchells rather. But, really, that's nothing. I think you'll be a little disappointed if you think he's at all of the romantic type."

"I didn't think that," she answered, though of course she had; "but something told me—I don't know why—that there's some strange attraction. . . I never saw a more perfect wife than you, nor a more perfect mother. But these things should be nipped in the bud, dear. They get hold of you sometimes before you know where you are. And think," she went on with relish, "how terrible it would be practically to break up two homes!"

"Oh, really, I must stop you there," cried Edith. "You don't think of elopements, do you?"

"I don't say that, necessarily. But I've seen a great deal of life. I've lived everywhere, and just the very households—*ménages,* as we say abroad—that seem most calm and peaceful, sometimes—It would be, anyhow, very dreadful, wouldn't it—to live a double life?"

Edith thought her friend rather enjoyed the idea, but she said:

"You don't imagine, I hope, that there's anything in the nature of an intrigue going on between me and Mr. Mitchell?"

"No, no, no—not now—not yet—but you don't quite know, Edith, how one can be carried away. As I was sitting up in my room—thinking—"

"You think too much," interrupted Edith.

"Perhaps so—but it came to me like this. I mean to be the one to put things right again, if I can. My dear child, a woman of the world like myself sees things. You two ought to be ideally happy. You're meant for one another—I mean you and Bruce."

"Do you think so?"

"Absolutely. But this—what shall I say?—this fascination is coming between you, and, though you don't realise it, it's saddening Bruce's life; it will sadden yours too. At first, no doubt, at the stage you're in, dear, it seems all romance and excitement. But later on—Now, Edith, promise me you won't be angry with me for what I've said? It's a terrible freedom that I've taken, I know. Really a liberty. But if I were your"— she glanced at the mirror—"elder sister, I couldn't be fonder of you. Don't think I'm a horrid, interfering old thing, will you?"

"Indeed I don't; you're a dear."

"Well, we won't speak of it any more till after Tuesday," said Madame Frabelle, "and take my advice: throw yourself into other things."

She glanced round the room.

"It's a splendid idea to divert your thoughts; why don't you refurnish your boudoir?"

Edith had often noticed the strange lack in Eglantine of any sense of decoration. She dressed charmingly, but with regard to surroundings she was entirely devoid of taste. She had the curious provincialism so often seen in cosmopolitans who have lived most of their lives in hotels, without apparently noticing or caring about their surroundings.

Edith made rather a hobby of decoration, and she had a cultured and quiet taste, and much knowledge on the subject. She guessed Madame Frabelle thought her rooms too plain, too colourless. Instead of the dull greys and blues, and surfaces without design, she felt sure her friend would have preferred gorgeous patterns, and even a good deal of gilt. Probably at heart Madame Frabelle's ideal was the crimson plush and stamped leather and fancy ceilings of the lounge in a foreign hotel.

"I rather like my room, you know," said Edith.

"And so do I. It's very charming. But a change, dear—a change of *entourage*, as we say abroad, would do you good."

"Well, we must really think that out," said Edith.

"That's right. And you're not cross?"

"Cross? I don't know when I've enjoyed a conversation so much," said Edith, speaking with perfect truth.

V

The Ottleys and Madame Frabelle were in the drawing-room awaiting their guests. (I say advisedly their guests, for no-one could help regarding Madame Frabelle as essentially the hostess, and queen of the evening.) One would fancy that instead of entertaining more or less for the last twelve years the young couple had never given a dinner before; so much suppressed excitement was in the air. Bruce was quiet and subdued now from combined nervousness and pride, but for the few days previous he had been terribly trying to his unfortunate wife; nothing, according to him, could be good enough for the purpose of impressing Madame Frabelle, and he appeared to have lost all his confidence in Edith's undeniable gift for receiving.

The flowers, the menu, the arrangement of the eight people—for the dinner was still small, intimate and distinguished, as he had first suggested—had been subjected to continual and maddening changes in its scheme. Everyone had been disengaged and everyone had accepted—then he wished he had asked other people instead.

When Edith was dressed Bruce put the last touch to his irritating caprices by asking Edith to take out of her hair a bandeau of blue that he had first asked her to put in. Every woman will know what agony that must have caused. The pretty fair hair was waved and arranged specially for this ornament, and when she took it out the whole scheme seemed to her wrong. However, she looked very pretty, dressed in vaporous tulle of a shade of blue which only a faultless complexion can bear.

Edith's complexion was her strong point. When she was a little flushed she looked all the better for it, and when she was pale it seemed to suit her none the worse. Hers was the sort of skin with a satiny texture that improves under bright sunshine or electric light; in fact the more brilliantly it was lighted the better it looked.

Madame Frabelle (of course) was dressed in black, *décolletée*, and with a good deal of jet. A black aigrette, like a lightning conductor, stood up defiantly in her hair. Though it did not harmonise well with the somewhat square and *bourgeois* shape of her head and face, and appeared to have dropped on her by accident, yet as a symbol of smartness it gave her a kind of distinction. It appeared to have fallen from the skies; it was put on in the wrong place, and it did not nestle, as it should do, and appear to grow out of the hair, since that glory of womanhood, in her case of a dull brown, going slightly grey, was smooth, scarce and plainly parted. Madame Frabelle really would have looked her best in a cap of the fashion of the sixties. But she could carry off anything; and some people said that she did.

Edith had been allowed by her husband *carte blanche* in the decoration of their house.

This was fortunate, as *mise-en-scène* was a great gift of hers; no-one had such a sense as Edith for arranging a room. She had struck the happy mean between the eccentric and the conventional. Anything that seemed unusual did not appear to be a pose, or a strained attempt at being different from others, but seemed to have a reason of its own. For example, she greatly disliked the usual gorgeous *endimanché* drawing-room and dark conventional dining-room. The room in which she received her guests was soft and subdued in colour and not dazzling with that blaze of light that is so trying to strangers just arrived and not knowing their way about a house (or certain of how they are looking). The room seemed to receive them kindly; make them comfortable, and at their ease, hoping they looked best. The shaded lights, not dim enough to be depressing, were kind to those past youth and gave confidence to the shy. There was nothing ceremonious, nothing chilly, about the drawing-room; it was essentially at once comfortable and becoming, and the lights shone like shaded sunshine from the dull pink corners of the room.

On the other hand, the dining-room helped conversation by its stimulating gaiety and daintiness.

The feminine curves of the furniture, such as is usually kept for the drawing-room, were all pure Louis-Quinze. It was deliriously pretty in its pink and white and pale green.

In the drawing-room the hosts stood by one of those large, old-fashioned oaken fireplaces so supremely helpful to conversation and *tête-à-têtes*. In Edith's house there was never any general conversation except at dinner. People simply made friends, flirted, and enjoyed themselves.

As the clock struck eight the Mitchells were announced. Edith could scarcely control a laugh as Mr. Mitchell came in, he looked so utterly unlike the dangerous lover Madame Frabelle had conjured up. He was immensely tall, broad, loosely built, large-shouldered, with a red beard, a twinkle in his eye, and the merriest of laughs. He was a delightful man, but there was no romance about him. Besides, Edith remembered him as a black poodle.

Mrs. Mitchell struck a useful note, and seemed a perfect complement to her husband, the ideal wife for him. She was about forty-five, but being slim, animated, and well dressed (though entirely without *chic*), she seemed a good deal younger.

Mr. Mitchell might have been any age between sixty and sixty-five, and had the high spirits and vitality of a boy.

It was impossible to help liking this delightful couple; they fully deserved their popularity. In the enormous house at Hampstead, arranged like a country mansion, where they lived, Mr. Mitchell made it the object of his life to collect Bohemians as other people collect Venetian glass, from pure love of the material. His wife, with a silly woman's subtlety, having rather lower ideals—that is to say, a touch of the very human vulgarity known as social ambition—made use of his Bohemianism to help her on in her mundane success. This was the principle of the thing. If things were well done—and they always were at her house—would not a duke, if he were musical, go anywhere to hear the greatest tenor in Europe? And would not all the greatest celebrities go anywhere to meet a duke?

Next the two young Conistons were announced.

Miss Coniston was a thin, amiable, artistic girl, who did tooling in leather, made her own dresses, recited, and had a pale, good-looking, too well-dressed, disquieting young brother of twenty-two, who seemed to be always going out when other people came in, but was rather useful in society, being musical and very polite. The music that he chose generally gave his audience a shock. Being so young, so pale, and so contemporary, one expected him to sing thin, elusive music by Debussy, Fauré, or Ravel. He seemed never to have heard of these composers, but sang instead threatening songs, such as, "I'll sing thee Songs of Araby!" or defiant, teetotal melodies, like "Drink to Me only with thine Eyes!" His voice was good, and louder and deeper than one would expect. He accompanied himself and his sister everywhere. She, by the way, to add to the interest about her, was said to be privately engaged to a celebrity who was never there. Alice and Guy Coniston were orphans, and lived alone in a tiny flat in Pelham Gardens. He had been reading for the Bar, but when the war broke out he joined the New Army, and was now in khaki.

But the *clou* and great interest of the evening was the arrival of Sir Tito Landi, that most popular of all Italian composers. With his white moustache, pink and white complexion, and large bright blue eyes, his dandified dress, his eyeglass and buttonhole, he had the fresh, fair look of an Englishman, the dry brilliance of a Parisian, the *naïveté* of a genius, the manners of a courtier, and behind it all the diabolic humour of the Neapolitan. He was small, thin and slight, with a curious dignity of movement.

"Ah, Tito," cried Bruce cordially. "Here you are!"

The dinner was bright and gay from the very beginning, even before the first glass of champagne. It began with an optimistic view of the war, then, dropping the grave subject, they talked of people, theatres, books, and general gossip. In all these things Madame Frabelle took the lead. Indeed, she had begun at once laying down the law in a musical voice but with a determined manner that gave those who knew her to understand only too well that she intended to go steadily on, and certainly not to stop to breathe before the ices.

Sir Tito Landi, fixing his eyeglass in his bright blue eye, took in Madame Frabelle in one long look, and smiled at her sympathetically.

"What do you think of her?" murmured Edith to Landi.

Hypnotised and slightly puzzled as she was by her guest, she was particularly curious for his opinion, as she knew him to be the best judge of character of her acquaintance. He had some of the capriciousness of the spoilt, successful artist, which showed itself, except to those whom he regarded as real friends, in odd variations of manner, so that Edith could not tell at all by his being extremely charming to Madame Frabelle that he liked her, or by his being abrupt and satirical that he didn't. An old friend and a favourite, she could rely on what he told her.

"C'est une bonne vieille," he said. "Bonne, mais bête!"

"Really?" Edith asked, surprised.

Landi laughed. "Bête comme ses pieds, ma chère!"

Returning to decent language and conventional tone, he went on with a story he was telling about an incident that had happened when he was staying with some royalties. His stories were short, new, amusing, and invariably suited to his audience. Anything about the Court he saw, at a glance, would genuinely interest Madame Frabelle. Edith was amused as she saw that lady becoming more and more convinced of Landi's importance, and of his respectful admiration.

Long before dinner was over there was no doubt that everyone was delighted with Madame Frabelle. She talked so well, suited herself to everyone, and simply charmed them all. Yet why? Edith was still wondering, but by the time she rose to go upstairs she thought she began to understand her friend's secret. People were not charmed with Eglantine because she herself was charming, but because she was charmed. Madame Frabelle was really as much interested in everyone to whom she spoke as she appeared to be; the interest was not assumed. A few little pretences and affectations she might have, such as that of knowing a great deal about every subject under the sun—of having read everything, and been everywhere, but her interest in other people was real. That was what made people like her.

Young Coniston, shy, sensitive and reserved as he was, had nevertheless told her all about his training at Braintree, the boredom of getting up early, the dampness of the tents, and how much he wanted to be sent to the front. She admired his valour, was interested in his music, and at her persuasion he promised to sing her songs of Araby after dinner.

When the ladies were alone Eglantine's universal fascination was even more remarkable. Mrs. Mitchell, at her desire, gave her the address of the little dressmaker who ran up Mrs. Mitchell's blouses and skirts. This was an honour for Mrs. Mitchell; nothing pleased her so much as to be asked for the address of her dressmaker by a woman with a foreign name.

As to Miss Coniston, she was enraptured with Eglantine. Madame Frabelle arranged to go and see her little exhibition of tooled leather, and coaxed out of the shy girl various details about the celebrity, who at present had an ambulance in France. She adored reciting, and Miss Coniston, to gratify her, offered to recite a poem by Emile Cammaerts on the spot.

As to Mr. Mitchell, Madame Frabelle drew him out with more care and caution. With the obstinacy of the mistaken she still saw in Mr. Mitchell's friendly looks at his hostess a passion for Edith, and shook her grey head over the blindness of the poor dear wife.

Bruce hung on her words and was open-mouthed while she spoke, so impressed was he at her wonderful cleverness, and at her evident success with his friends.

Later on Landi, sitting in the ingle-nook with Edith, said, as he puffed a cigar:

"Tiens, ma chère Edith, tu ne vois pas quelque chose?"

"What?"

He always talked French, as a middle course between Italian and English, and Edith spoke her own language to him.

"Elle. La Mère Frabelle," he laughed to himself. "Elle est folle de ton mari!"

"Oh, really, Landi! That's your fancy!"

He mimicked her. "Farncy! Farncy! Je me suis monté l'imagination, peut-être! J'ai un rien de fièvre, sans doute! C'est une idée que j'ai, comme ça. Eh bien! Non! Nous verrons. Je te dis qu'elle est amoureuse de Bruce."

"He is very devoted to her, I know," said Edith, "and I daresay he's a little in love with her—in a way. But she—"

"C'est tout le contraire, chère. Lui, c'est moins; il est flatté. Il la trouve une femme intelligente," he laughed. "Mais elle! Tu est folle de ne pas voir ça, Edith. Enfin! Si ça l'amuse?"

With a laugh he got up, to loud applause, and went to the little white enamelled piano. There, with a long cigar in his mouth, he struck a few notes, and at once magnetised his audience. The mere touch of his fingers on the piano thrilled everyone present.

He sang a composition of his own, which even the piano-organ had never succeeded in making hackneyed, "Adieu, Hiver," and melodious as only Italian music can be. Blue beams flashed from his eyes; he seemed in a dream. Suddenly in the most impassioned part, which he was singing in a composer's voice, that is, hardly any voice, but with perfect art, he caught Madame Frabelle's eye, and gave her a solemn wink. She burst out laughing. He then went on singing with sentiment and grace.

All the women present imagined that he was making love to them, while each man felt that he, personally, was making love to his ideal woman. Such was the effect of Landi's music. It made the most material, even the most unmusical, remember some little romance, some *tendresse*, some sentiment of the past; Landi seemed to get at the soft spot in everybody's heart. All the audience looked dreamy. Edith was thinking of Aylmer Ross. Where was he now? Would she ever see him again? Had she been wise to throw away her happiness like that? She tried to put the thought aside, but she observed, with a smile, that Madame Frabelle looked—and not when he was looking at her—a shade tenderly at Bruce.

Edith remembered what Landi had said: "Si ça l'amuse?" She found an opportunity to tell him that Madame Frabelle believed in her own intuitions, and had got it into her head that she and Mr. Mitchell were attached to one another.

"Naturellement. Elle veut s'excuser; la pauvre."

"But she really believes it."

"Elle voit double, alors!" exclaimed Landi.

VI

E dith and Madame Frabelle had long talks next day over the little dinner-party, and the people of their intimate circle whom she had met. She was delighted with Landi, though a little frightened of him, as most people were when they first knew him, unless he really liked them immensely.

She impressed on Edith to beware of Mr. Mitchell.

Bruce, for once, had really been satisfied with his own entertainment, and declared to Edith that Madame Frabelle had made it go off splendidly.

Edith was growing to like her more and more. In a house where Bruce lived it was certainly a wonderful help to have a third person often present—if it was the right person. The absurd irritations and scenes of fault-finding that she had become inured to, but which were always trying, were now shorter, milder, or given up altogether. Bruce's temper was perennially good, and got better. Then the constant illnesses that he used to suffer from—he was unable to pass the military examination and go to the front on account of a neurotic heart—these illnesses were either omitted entirely or talked over with Madame Frabelle, whose advice turned out more successful than that of a dozen specialists.

"An extraordinary woman she is, you know, Edith," he said. "You know that really peculiar feeling I sometimes have?"

"Which, dear?"

"You know that sort of emptiness in the feet, and heaviness in the head, and that curious kind of twitching of the eyelids that I get?"

"Yes, I know. Well, dear?"

"Well, Madame Frabelle has given me a complete cure for it. It seems her husband (by the way, what a brute he must have been, and what a life that poor woman led! However, never mind that now) had something very much of the same kind, only not quite so bad."

"Which, dear?"

"How do you mean 'Which'? Which what?"

"Which peculiar feeling?"

"What peculiar feeling are we talking about?"

"I said, which peculiar feeling did Mr. Frabelle have?"

"What are you trying to get at, Edith?" He looked at her suspiciously. Edith sighed.

"Was it the heaviness in the feet, or the lightness in the head, or was it the twitching of the eyelid which Mr. Frabelle used to suffer from?"

"Oh, ah! Yes, I see what you mean. It seemed he had a little of them all. But what do you think she used to do?"

"I haven't the slightest idea."

"There's some stuff called Tisane—have you ever heard of it?" Bruce asked. "It's a simple remedy, but a very good thing. Well, he used to use that."

"Did he bathe his eye with it?"

"Oh, my dear Edith, you're wool-gathering. Do pull yourself together. He drank it, that's what he did, and that's what I'm going to do. Eg— Madame Frabelle would go straight down into the kitchen and show you how to make it if you like."

"I don't mind, if cook doesn't," said Edith.

"Oh, we'll see about that. Anyway she's going to show me how to get it made."

"Then there's another thing Madame Frabelle suggested. She's got an idea it would do me a world of good to spend a day in the country."

"Oh, really? Sounds a good idea."

"Yes. Say, on the river. She's not been there for years it seems. She thinks she would rather enjoy it."

"I should think it would be a capital plan," said Edith.

"Well, how about next Saturday?" said Bruce, thinking he was concealing his eagerness and satisfaction.

"Saturday? Oh yes, certainly. Saturday, by all means, if it's fine. What time shall we start?"

He started at once, but was silent.

"Saturday, yes," Edith went on, after a glance at him. "Only, I promised to take the two children to an afternoon performance."

"Did you though?" Bruce brightened up. "Rather hard luck on them to disappoint them. Mind you, Edith, I don't believe in spoiling children. I don't think their parents should be absolute slaves to them; but, on the other hand, I don't think it's good for them to disappoint them quite so much as that; and, after all—well, a promise to a child!" He shook his head sentimentally. "Perhaps it's a fad of mine; I daresay it is; but I don't like the idea of breaking a promise to a child!"

"It does seem a shame. Too bad."

"You agree with me? I knew you would. I've heard you say the same yourself. Well then, look here, Edith; suppose we do it—suppose you do it, I mean. Suppose you go with Archie and Dilly. They're to lunch with my mother, aren't they?"

"Yes, dear. But we were to have fetched them from there and then taken them on to the theatre!"

"Well, do it, then, my dear girl! Stick to your plan. Don't let me spoil your afternoon! Gracious heaven! I—I—why, I can quite well take Madame Frabelle myself." He looked at the barometer. "The glass is going up," he said, giving it first a tap and then a slight shake to encourage it to go up higher and to look sharp about it. "So that's settled, then, dear. That's fixed up. I'll take her on the river. I don't mind in the very least. I shall be only too pleased—delighted. Oh, don't thank me, my dear girl; I know one ought to put oneself out for a guest, especially a widow. . . under these circumstances over in England. . . during the war too. . . hang it, it's the least one can do." . . . Bruce's murmurings were interrupted by the entrance of the lady in question. He made the suggestion, and explained the arrangement. She consented immediately with much graciousness.

"I dote on the river, and haven't been for years."

"Now where would you like to go?" he asked. "What part of the river do you like? How about Maidenhead?"

"Oh, any part. Don't ask me! Anything you suggest is sure to be right. You know far more about these things than I do. But Maidenhead—isn't it just a little commonplace? A little noisy and crowded, even now?"

"By jove, yes, you're quite right. Madame Frabelle's perfectly right, Edith, you know. Well, what about Shepperton?"

"Shepperton? Oh, charming! Dear little town. But it isn't exactly what I call the river, if you know what I mean. I mean to say—"

"Well, could you suggest a place?" said Bruce.

"Oh, I'm the worst person in the world for suggesting anything," said Madame Frabelle. "And I know so little of the river. But how about Kingston?"

"Kingston? Oh, capital. That would be charming."

"Kyngestown, as it used to be called" (Madame Frabelle hastened to show her knowledge) "in the days when Saxon kings were crowned there. Am I wrong or not? Oh, surely yes. . . Wasn't it Kingston? Didn't great Caesar cross the river there? And the Roman legions camp upon the sloping uplands?"

Bruce gasped. "You know everything!" he exclaimed.

"Oh no. I remember a little about the history," she said modestly, "Ah, poor, weak King Edwy!"

"Yes, indeed," said Bruce, though he had no recollection of having heard the gentleman mentioned before. "Poor chap!"

"Too bad," murmured Edith.

"How he must have hated that place!" said Madame Frabelle.

"Rather. I should think so indeed."

"However, *you* won't," said Edith adroitly changing the subject, seeing her husband getting deeper out of his depth.

Most of the evening Madame Frabelle read up Baedeker, to the immense astonishment of Bruce, who had never before thought of regarding the river from the historical and geographical point of view.

The next day, which was fine, if not warm, the two started off with a certain amount of bustle and a bundle of rugs, Madame Frabelle in a short skirt with a maritime touch about the collar and what she called a suitable hat and a dark blue motor veil. She carried off the whole costume to admiration.

Archie seemed rather bewildered and annoyed at this division of the party.

"But, Mother, we're going out to lunch with grandmother."

"I know, darling. I'll come and fetch you from there."

Conventional and restrained as Archie usually was, he sometimes said curious things.

Edith saw by his dreamy expression he was going to say one now.

He looked at her for a little while after his father's departure and then asked:

"Mother!"

"Yes, darling."

"Is Madame Frabelle a nice little friend for father?"

Edith knew he had often heard her and the nurse or the governess discussing whether certain children were nice little friends for him or Dilly.

"Oh yes, dear, very nice."

"Oh."

The cook came in for orders.

"You're going to lunch all alone then, aren't you, Mother?"

"Yes, I suppose I must. I don't mind. I've got a nice book."

Archie walked slowly to the door, then said in a tone of envious admiration which contained a note of regret:

"I suppose you'll order a delicious pudding?"

SHE WENT TO FETCH THE children, who were excited at the prospect of a theatre. The elder Mrs. Ottley was a pleasant woman, who understood and was utterly devoted to her daughter-in-law. Fond as she was of her son, she marvelled at Edith's patience and loved her as much as she loved Bruce. Though she had never been told, for she was the sort of woman who does not require to be told things in order to know them, she knew every detail of the sacrifice Edith had once made. She had been almost as charmed by Aylmer Ross as her daughter-in-law was, and she had considered Edith's action nearly sublime. But she had never believed Edith was at that time really in love with Aylmer. She had said, after Bruce's return: "It mustn't happen again, you know, Edith."

"What mustn't?"

"Don't spoil Bruce. You've made it almost too easy for him. Don't let him think he can always be running away and coming back!"

"No, never again," Edith had answered, with a laugh.

Now they never spoke of the subject. It was a painful one to Mrs. Ottley.

Today that lady seemed inclined to detain Edith, and make her—as Archie feared—late for the rising of the curtain.

"You really like Madame Frabelle so much, dear?"

"Really I do," said Edith. "The more I know her, the more I like her. She's the most good-natured, jolly, kind woman I've ever seen. Landi likes her too. That's a good sign."

"And she keeps Bruce in a good temper?" said Mrs. Ottley slyly.

"Well, why shouldn't she? I'm not afraid of Madame Frabelle," Edith said, laughing. "After all, Bruce may be thirty-seven, but she's fifty."

"She's a wonderful woman," admitted Mrs. Ottley, who had at first disliked her, but had come round, like everyone else. "Very very nice; and really I do like her. But you know my old-fashioned ideas. I never approve of a third person living with a married couple."

"Oh—living! She's only been with us about a month."

"But you don't think she's going away before the end of the season?"

"You can't call it a season. And she can't easily settle down just now, on account of the war. Many of her relations are abroad, and some in the country. She hasn't made up her mind where to live yet. She has never had a house of her own since her husband died."

"Yes, I see."

"Do come, Mother!" urged Archie.

"All right, darling."

"Will I have to take my hat off?" pouted Dilly, who had on a new hat with daisies round it, in which she looked like a baby angel. She had a great objection to removing it.

"Yes, dear. Why should you mind?"

"My hair will be all anyhow if I have to take it off in the theatre," said Dilly.

"Don't be a silly little ass," Archie murmured to his sister. "Why, in some countries women would be sent to prison unless they took their hats off at a play!"

The three reached the theatre in what even Archie called good time. This meant to be alone in the dark, gloomy theatre for at least twenty minutes, no-one present as yet, except two or three people eating oranges in the gallery. He liked to be the first and the last.

Edith was fancying to herself how Madame Frabelle would lay down the law about the history of Kingston, and read portions of the guide-book aloud, while Bruce was pointing out the scenery.

The entertainment, which was all odds and ends, entertained the children, but rather bored her. Archie was learning by heart—which was a way he had—the words of a favourite song now being sung—

> *"Kitty, Kitty, isn't it a pity,*
> *In the city you work so hard,—*
> *With your one, two, three, four, five,*
> *Six, three, seven, five, Cerrard?*
>
> *Kitty, Kitty, isn't it a pity,*
> *That you're wasting so much time?*
> *With your lips close to the telephone,*
> *When they might be close to mine!"*

When Edith's eye was suddenly attracted by the appearance of a boy in khakis, who was in a box to her right. He looked about seventeen and was tall and good-looking; but what struck her about him was his remarkable likeness in appearance and in movement to Aylmer Ross. Even his back reminded her strongly of her hero. There was something familiar in the thick, broad shoulders, in the cool ease of manner, and in the expression of the face. But could that young man—why, of course, it was three years ago when she parted with Aylmer Ross, Teddy was fourteen; these years made a great difference and of course all plans had been changed on account of the war. Aylmer, she thought, was too old to have been at the front. The boy must be in the New Army.

She watched him perpetually; she felt a longing to go and speak to him. After a while, as though attracted by her interest, he turned round and looked her straight in the face. How thrilled she felt at this likeness. . . They were the very last to go out, and Edith contrived to be near the party in the box. She dropped something and the young man picked it up. She had never seen him, and yet she felt she knew him. When he smiled she could not resist speaking to him.

"Thank you. Excuse me. Are you the son of Mr. Aylmer Ross?"

"I am. And I know you quite well by your photograph," he said in exactly Aylmer's pleasant, casual voice. "You were a great friend of my father's, weren't you?"

"Yes. Where are you now?"

He was at Aldershot, but was in town on leave.

"And where's your father?"

"Didn't you know? My father's at the front. He's coming over on leave, too, in a fortnight."

"Really? And are you still at Jermyn Street?"

"Oh yes. Father let his house for three years, but we've come back again. Jolly little house, isn't it?"

"Very. And I hope we shall see you both," said Edith conventionally.

The boy bowed, smiled and walked away so quickly that Archie had no time for the salute he had prepared.

He was wonderfully like Aylmer.

Edith was curiously pleased and excited about this little incident.

VII

Madame Frabelle and Bruce arrived at Waterloo in good time for the 11.10 train, which Bruce had discovered in the ABC.

They wished to know where it started, but nobody appeared interested in the subject. Guards and porters, of whom they inquired, seemed surprised at their questions and behaved as if they regarded them as signs of vulgar and impertinent curiosity. At Waterloo no-one seems to know when a train is going to start, where it is starting from, or where it is going to. Madame Frabelle unconsciously assumed an air of embarrassment, as though she had no responsibility for the queries and excited manner of her companion. She seemed, indeed, surprised when Bruce asked to see the station-master. Here things came to a head. There was no train for Kingston at 11.10; the one at that hour was the Southampton Express; and it was worse than useless for Bruce and Madame Frabelle.

"Then the ABC and Bradshaw must both be wrong," said Bruce reproachfully to Madame Frabelle.

An idea occurred to that resourceful lady. "Perhaps the 11.10 was only to start on other days, not on Saturdays."

She turned out to be right. However, they discovered a train at twenty minutes to twelve, which would take them where they wanted, though it was not mentioned, apparently, in any timetable, and could only be discovered by accident by someone who was looking for something else.

They hung about the station until it arrived, feeling awkward and uncomfortable, as people do when they have arrived too early for a train. Meanwhile they abused Bradshaw, and discussed the weather. Bruce said how wonderful it was how some people always knew what sort of weather it was going to be. Madame Frabelle, who was getting sufficiently irritable to be epigrammatic, said that she never cared to know what the weather was going to be; the weather in England was generally bad enough when it came without the added misery of knowing about it beforehand.

Bruce complained that she was too Continental. He very nearly said that if she didn't like England he wondered she hadn't remained in France, but he stopped himself.

At last the train arrived. Bruce had settled his companion with her back to the engine in a corner of a first-class carriage, and placed her rugs in the rack above. As they will on certain days, every little thing went wrong, and the bundle promptly fell off. As she moved to catch it, it tumbled on to her hat, nearly crushing the crown. Unconsciously assuming the expression of a Christian martyr, Madame Frabelle said it didn't matter. Bruce had given her *The Gentlewoman*, *The World*, *The Field*, *Punch*, and *The London Mail* to occupy the twenty-five minutes or so while they waited for the train to start. The journey itself was much shorter than this interval. Knowing her varied interests, he felt sure that these journals would pretty well cover the ground, but he was rather surprised, as he took the seat opposite her, to see that she read first, in fact instantly started, with apparent interest, on *The London Mail*. With a quick glance he saw that she was enjoying "What Everybody Wants to Know"—"Why the Earl of Blank looked so surprised when he met the pretty little blonde lady who had been said to be the friend of his wife walking in Bond Street with a certain dark gentleman who until now he had always understood to be her *bête noire*," and so forth.

As an example to her he took up *The New Statist* and read a serious article.

When they arrived it was fine and sunny, and they looked at once for a boat.

It had not occurred to him before that there would be any difficulty in getting one. He imagined a smart new boat all ready for him, with fresh, gay cushions, and everything complete and suitable to himself and his companion. He was rather irritated when he found instead that the best they could do for him was to give him a broken-down, battered-looking thing like an old chest, which was to be charged rather heavily for the time they meant to spend on the river. It looked far from safe, but it was all they could do. So they got in. Bruce meant to show his powers as an oarsman. He said Madame Frabelle must steer and asked her to trim the boat.

In obedience to his order she sat down with a bang, so heavily that Bruce was nearly shot up into the air. Amiable as she always was, and respectfully devoted as Bruce was to her, he found that being on the river has a mysterious power of bringing out any defects of temper that people have concealed when on dry ground. He said to her:

"Don't do that again. Do you mind?" as politely as he could.

She looked up, surprised.

"I beg your pardon, Mr. Ottley?"

"Don't do that again."

"Don't do what? What did I do?"

"Why, I asked you to trim the boat."

"What did I do? I merely sat down."

He didn't like to say that she shouldn't sit down with a bump, and took his place.

"If you like," she said graciously, "I'll relieve you there, presently."

"How do you mean—relieve me?"

"I mean I'll row—I'll sit in the stern—row!"

"Perhaps you've forgotten the names of the different parts of a boat. Madame Frabelle?"

"Oh, I think not, Mr. Ottley. It's a good while since I was on the river, but it's not the sort of thing one forgets, and I'm supposed to have rather a good memory."

"I'm sure you have—a wonderful memory—still, where I'm sitting is not the stern."

There was a somewhat sulky silence. They admired the scenery of the river. Madame Frabelle said she loved the distant glimpses of the grey old palace of the Tudors, and asked him if he could imagine what it was like when it was gay all day with the clanking of steel and prancing horses and things.

"How I love Hampton Court!" she said. "It looks so quiet and peaceful. I think I should like to live there. Think of the evenings in that wonderful old place, with its panelled walls, and the echo of feet that are no longer there, down the cold, stone corridors—"

Bruce gave a slight laugh.

"Echo of feet that are no longer there? But how could that be? Dear me, how poetical you are, Madame Frabelle!"

"I mean the imaginary echo."

"Imaginary—ah, yes. You're very imaginative, aren't you, Madame Frabelle? Well, I don't know whether it's imagination or not, but, do you know, I fancy that queer feeling of mine seems to be coming on again."

"What queer feeling?"

"I told you about it, and you were very sympathetic the other night, before dinner. A kind of emptiness in the feet, and a hollowness in the head, the feeling almost, but not quite, of faintness."

"It's nearly two o'clock. Perhaps you're hungry," said Madame Frabelle.

Bruce thought this was not fair, putting all the hunger on to him, as if she had never felt anything so prosaic. Madame Frabelle always behaved as if she were superior to the weaknesses of hunger or sleep, and denied ever suffering from either.

"It may be. I had no breakfast," said Bruce untruthfully, as though it were necessary to apologise for requiring food to sustain life.

"Nor did I," said Madame Frabelle hastily.

"Well, don't you feel that you would like a little lunch?"

"Oh no—oh dear, no. Still, I dare say some food would do you good, Mr. Ottley—keep you up. I'll come and watch you."

"But you must have something too."

"Must I? Oh, very well, just to keep you company."

They got out very briskly, and, leaving their battered-looking coffin (called ironically the *Belle of the River*), they walked with quick steps to the nearest hotel. Here they found a selection of large, raw-looking cold beef, damp, tired-looking ham, bread, cheese, celery, and dessert in the form of dry apples, oranges, and Brazil nuts that had long left their native land.

Bruce decided that the right thing to drink was shandy-gaff, but, to keep up her Continental reputation, Madame Frabelle said she would like a little light wine of the country.

"Red, white, or blue?" asked Bruce, whose spirits were rising.

She laughed very heartily, and decided on a little red.

They had an adequate, if not exquisite, lunch, then Madame Frabelle said she would like to go over Hampton Court. A tedious guide offered to go with them, but Madame Frabelle said she knew all about the place better than he did, so they wandered through the beautiful old palace.

"Oh, to think of King Charles II's beauties living there—those lovely, languid ladies—how charming they were!" exclaimed Madame Frabelle.

"They wore very low dresses," said Bruce, who felt rather sleepy and stupid, and as if he didn't quite know what he was saying.

Madame Frabelle modestly looked away from the pictures.

"How exquisite the garden is."

He agreed, and they went out and sat, somewhat awkwardly, on an uncomfortable stone seat.

There was a delicious half-hour of real summer sun—"One of those April days that seem a forecast of June," as Madame Frabelle said.

"How much better it is to be here in the beautiful fresh air than squeezed into a stuffy theatre," remarked Bruce, who was really feeling a shade jealous of Edith for seeing the revue that he had wished to see.

"Yes, indeed. There's nothing like England, I think," she said rather irrelevantly.

"How exactly our tastes agree."

"Do they?"

Her hand was on the edge of the seat. Somehow or other Bruce's had gone over it. She didn't appear to notice it.

"What small hands you have!" he remarked.

"Oh no! I take sixes," said the lady, whose size was really three-quarters more than that.

He insisted on looking at the grey suède glove, and then examined her rings.

"I suppose these rings have—er—associations for you, Madame Frabelle?"

"Ah!" she said, shaking her head. "This one—yes, this one—the sapphire recalls old memories." She sighed; she had bought it in the Brompton Road.

"A present from your husband, I suppose?" said Bruce, with a tinge of bitterness.

"Ah!" she answered.

She thought he was getting a little sentimental, too early in the day, and, with an effort at energy, she said:

"Let's go back to the river."

They went back, and now Bruce began to show off his rowing powers. He had not practised for a long time, and didn't get along very quickly. She admired his athletic talents, as though he had been a winner of the Diamond Sculls.

"If I'd stuck to it, you know," he said, rather apologetically, "I'd have done well in the rowing line. At one time—a good while ago—I thought of going in for Henley, in the Regatta, you know. But with that beastly Foreign Office one can't keep up anything of that sort."

"I suppose not."

"My muscle," said Bruce, sticking out his arm, and hitting it rather hard, "is fairly good, you know. Not bad for a London man who never has any practice."

"No indeed."

"My arm was about seventeen inches round just below the elbow at one time," Bruce said, "a few years ago."

"Just fancy! Splendid!" said Madame Frabelle, who remembered that her waist was not much more a good while ago.

He told her a good many anecdotes of his prowess in the past, until tea-time.

Madame Frabelle depended greatly on tea; anything else she could do without. But a cup of tea in the afternoon was necessary to her well-being, and her animation. She became rather drowsy and absent by four o'clock.

Bruce again suggested their landing and leaving the *Belle of the River*, as they had not thought of bringing a tea-basket.

After tea, which was a great success, they became very cheery and jolly. They went for a walk and then back to their boat.

This was the happiest time of the day.

When they reached the station, about half-past six, they found a disagreeable crowd, pushing, screaming, and singing martial songs. As they got into their first-class carriage about a dozen third-class passengers sprang in, just as the train started. Bruce was furious, but nothing could be done, and the journey back to town was taken with Madame Frabelle very nearly pushed on to his knee by a rude young man who practically sat on hers, smoking a bad cigarette in her face.

They tacitly agreed to say nothing about this, and got home in time for dinner, declaring the day to have been a great success.

Bruce had really enjoyed it. Madame Frabelle said she had; though she had a certain little tenderness, half of a motherly kind, for Bruce, she far preferred his society in a comfortable house. She didn't really think he was ideal companion for the open air. And he was struck, as he had often been before, by her curious way of contradicting herself in conversation. She took any side and argued in favour of it so long as it was striking or romantic. At one moment she would say with the greatest earnestness, for instance, that divorce should not be allowed. Marriage should be for ever, or not at all. At another moment she would argue in favour of that absurd contradiction in terms known as free love, *forgetting* that she had completely changed round since earlier in the conversation. This was irritating, but he was still impressed with her infallibility, and Edith remarked more every day how curious that infallibility was, and how safe it was to trust. Whenever Madame Frabelle knew that something was going to happen, it didn't, and whenever she had an intuition that something was going to occur, *then* it was pretty safe. It never would. In the same way she had only to look at a person to see them as they were not. This was so invariable it was really very convenient to have her in the house, for whatever she said was always wrong. One had *merely* to go by contraries and her prophecies were most useful.

"It's been jolly for you," Bruce said to Edith, "having a ripping time in town while I'm taking your visitors about to show them England."

"You wouldn't have cared for the theatre," she said. "But, fancy, I met Aylmer's son there—Aylmer Ross, you know. Aylmer himself is at the front. They have taken their old house again. He means to come back there."

"Well, I really can't help it," said Bruce rather fretfully. "*I* should be at the front if it weren't for my neurotic heart. The doctor wouldn't hear of passing me—at least one wouldn't. Any fellow who would have done so would be—not a careful man. However, I don't know that it wouldn't have been just as good to die for my country, and get some glory, as to die of heart trouble here." He sighed.

"Oh no, you won't," said Edith reassuringly; "you look the picture of health."

"I've got a bit of sunburn, I think," said Bruce, popping up to look in the glass. "Funny how I do catch the sun. I asked Dr. Pollock about it one day."

"Really—did you consult him about your sunburn?"

"Yes. What are you smiling at, He said it's caused by the extreme delicacy of the mucous membrane; nothing to be anxious about."

"I don't think I am anxious; not particularly. And don't worry, my dear boy; it's very becoming," said Edith.

Bruce patted her head, and gave her a kiss, smiling.

VIII

"We're lunching with the Mitchells today," said Edith.

"Oh yes. I remember. I'm looking forward to it," graciously said Madame Frabelle. "It's a pity your husband can't come, isn't it? Ah, you naughty girl, I don't believe you think so!" Madame Frabelle, archly shook her finger at Edith.

"Eglantine, have you really seriously talked yourself into thinking that Mr. Mitchell is anything to me?"

"I don't say, dear," said Madame Frabelle, sitting down comfortably, and bringing out her knitting, "that you yourself are aware of it. I don't say that you're in love with him, but that he is devoted to you anyone with half-an-eye can see. And some day," she shook her head, "some day your interest in him may take you by surprise."

"It is *your* interest in him that surprises me," said Edith. "He's a good friend, and we like him very much. But for anything else!—"

"If so, it's really rather wonderful," mused Eglantine, "that you've never had a thought, even the merest dream, beyond your husband; that it has never even occurred to you that anyone else might have suited your temperament better."

Edith dropped her book, and picked it up again. Her friend thought she saw, whether through stooping or what not, an increase of colour in her face.

"It isn't everyone," continued Madame Frabelle, "who would appreciate your husband as you do. To me he is a very charming man. I can understand his inspiring a feeling almost of motherly interest. I even feel sometimes," she laughed, "as if it would be a pleasure to look after him, take care of him. I think it would not have been a bad thing for him to have married a woman a little older than himself. But you, Edith, you're so young. You see, you might have made a mistake when you married him. You were a mere girl, and I could imagine some of his ways might irritate a very young woman."

After a moment she went on: "I suppose Bruce was very handsome when you married him?"

"Yes, he was. But he hasn't altered much."

"Yet, as I told you before, Edith, though I think you an ideal wife, you don't give me the impression of being in love with him. I hope you don't take this as an impertinence, my dear?"

"Not at all. And I'm not sure that I am."

"Yet your mother-in-law told me the other day that you had been such a marvellous wife to him. That you had even made sacrifices. You have never had anything to forgive, surely?"

"Oh no, never," hastily said Edith, fearing that Mrs. Ottley was a little inclined to be indiscreet.

"She told me that Bruce had been occasionally attracted—only very slightly—by other women, but that you were the only person he really cared for."

"Oh, I doubt if he ever thinks much of anyone else," said Edith.

A CHARACTERISTIC OF THE MITCHELLS' entertainments was that one always met there the people they had met, even for the first time, at one's own house. Here were the Conistons, and Landi, whom Edith was always delighted to see.

It was a large and gay lunch. Edith was placed some distance from Mr. Mitchell. Of course there was also a novelty—some lion or other was always at the Mitchells'. Today it consisted of a certain clergyman, called the Rev. Byrne Fraser, of whom Mrs. Mitchell and her circle were making much. He was a handsome, weary-looking man of whom more was supposed than could conveniently be said. His wife, who adored him, admitted that though he was an excellent husband, he suffered from rheumatism and religious doubts, which made him occasionally rather trying. There had been some story about him—nobody knew what it was. Madame Frabelle instantly took his side, and said she was sure he had been ill-treated, though she knew nothing whatever about it. She was placed next to him at table and began immediately on what she thought was his special subject.

"I understand that you're very modern in your views," she said, smiling.

"I!" he exclaimed in some surprise. "Really you are quite mistaken. I don't think I am at all."

"Really? Oh, I'm so glad—I've such a worship myself for tradition. I'm so thankful that you have, too."

"I don't know that I have," he said.

"It's true, then, what I heard—I felt it was the moment I looked at you, Mr. Fraser—I mean, that you're an atheist."

"A *what*?" he exclaimed, turning pale with horror. "Good heavens, Madame, do you know what my profession is?"

He seemed utterly puzzled by her. She managed, all the same, somehow or other to lure him into a conversation in which she *heartily* took his side. By the end of lunch they were getting on splendidly, though neither of them knew what they were talking about.

And this was one of the curious characteristics of Madame Frabelle. Nobody made so many gaffes, yet no-one got out of them so well. To use the lawyer's phrase, she used so many words that she managed to engulf her own and her interlocutor's ideas. No-one, perhaps, had ever talked so much nonsense seriously as she did that day, but the Rev. Byrne Fraser said she was a remarkable woman, who had read and thought deeply. Also he was enchanted with her interest in him, as everybody always was.

Edith thought she had heard Mr. Mitchell saying something to the others that interested her. She managed to get near him when the gentlemen joined them in the studio, as they called the large room where there was a stage, a piano, a parquet floor, and every possible arrangement for amusement. Madame Frabelle moved quickly away, supposing that Edith wished to speak to him for his sake, whereas really it was in order to have repeated something she thought she had heard at lunch.

"Did I hear you saying anything about your old friend, Aylmer Ross?" she asked.

"Yes, indeed. Haven't you heard? The poor fellow has been wounded. He was taken into hospital at once, fortunately, and he's getting better, and is going to be brought home almost immediately, to the same old house in Jermyn Street. I think his son is to meet him at the station today. We must all go and see him. Capital chap, Aylmer. I always liked him. He's travelled so much that—even before the war—I hadn't seen him for three years."

"Was the wound serious?" asked Edith, who had turned pale.

"They were anxious at first. Now he's out of danger. But, poor chap, I'm afraid he won't be able to move for a good while. His leg is broken. I hear he's got to be kept lying down two or three months."

"Qu'est ce qu'il y a, Edith?" asked Landi, who joined her.

"I've just heard some bad news," she said, "but don't speak about it." She told him.

"Bien. Du calme, mon enfant; du calme!"

"But, I'm anxious, Landi."

"Ça se voit!"

"Do you think—"

"Ce ne sera rien. It's the best thing that could happen to him. He'll be all right. . . I suppose you want to see him, Edith?"

"He may not wish to see me," said Edith.

"Oh yes, he will. You were the first person he thought of," answered Landi. "Why, my dear, you forget you treated him badly!"

"Then, if he'd treated *me* badly he wouldn't care to see me again, you mean?"

"C'est probable," said Landi, selecting with care a very large cigar from a box that was being handed round. "Now, be quite tranquil. I shall go and see him directly I leave here, and I'll let you hear every detail. Will that do?"

"Thanks, dear Landi! . . . But even if he wishes to see me, ought I to go?"

"That I don't know. But you will."

He lighted the long cigar.

IX

Next morning Edith, who always came down to breakfast, though somewhat late, found on her plate a letter from Lady Conroy, that most vague and forgetful of all charming Irishwomen. It said:

My Dear Mrs Ottley,

Do excuse my troubling you, but could you give me a little information? Someone has asked me about Madame Frabelle. I know that she is a friend of yours, and is staying with you, and I said so; also I have a sort of idea that she was, in some way, connected with you by marriage or relationship, but of that I was not quite sure. I fancy that it is due to you that I have the pleasure of knowing her, anyhow.

"Could you tell me who she was before she married? What her husband was, and anything else about her? That she is most charming and a very clever woman I know, of course, already. To say she is a friend of yours is enough to say that, but the rest I forget.

"Hoping you will forgive my troubling you, and that you are all very well, I remain, yours most sincerely.

Kathleen Conroy

"P.S.—I began to take some lessons in nursing when I came across a most charming and delightful girl, called Dulcie Clay. Do you happen to know her at all? Her father married again and she was not happy at home, and, having no money, she went in for nursing, seriously (not as I did), but I'm afraid she is not strong enough for the profession. Remember me to Madame Frabelle."

Edith passed the letter to Bruce.

"Isn't this too delightful?" she said; "and exactly like her? She sends Madame Frabelle to me with a letter of introduction, and then asks me who she is!"

"Well," said Bruce, who saw nothing of the absurdity of the situation, "Lady Conroy is a most charming person. It looks almost as if she wanted to decline responsibility. I wouldn't annoy her for the world. You must give her all the information she wants, of course."

"But all I know I only know from her."

"Exactly. Well, tell her what she told you. Madame Frabelle told us candidly she made her acquaintance at the hotel! But it's absurd to tell Lady Conroy that back! We can't!"

Edith found the original letter of introduction, after some searching, and wrote to Lady Conroy to say that she understood Madame Frabelle, who was no connection of hers, was a clever, interesting woman, who wished to study English life in her native land. She was "*of good family; she had been a Miss Eglantine Pollard, and was the widow of a well-to-do French wine merchant.*" (This was word for word what Lady Conroy had told her.) She went on to say that she "*believed Madame Frabelle had several friends and connections in London.*"

"The Mitchells, for instance," suggested Bruce.

"Yes, that's a good idea. '*She knows the Mitchells very well,*'" Edith went on writing. "'*I think you know them also; they are very great friends of ours. Mr. Mitchell is in the Foreign Office.*'"

"And the Conistons?" suggested Bruce.

"Yes. '*She knows the Conistons; the nice young brother and sister we are so fond of. She has other friends in London, I believe, but she has not troubled to look them up. The more one sees of her the more one likes her. She is most charming and amiable and makes friends wherever she goes. I don't think I know anything more than this, dear Lady Conroy. Yours very sincerely, Edith Ottley. P.S.—I have not met Miss Dulcie Clay.*'"

Bruce was satisfied with this letter. Edith herself thought it the most amusing letter she had ever written.

"The clergyman whom she met at lunch yesterday, by the way," said Bruce, "wouldn't it sound well to mention him?"

Edith good-naturedly laughed, and added to the letter: "'*The Rev. Byrne Fraser knows our friend also, and seems to like her.*'"

"The only thing is," said Bruce, after a moment's pause, "perhaps that might do her harm with Lady Conroy, although he's a clergyman. There have been some funny stories about the Rev. Byrne Fraser."

"He certainly liked her," said Edith. "He wrote her a long letter last night, after meeting her at lunch, to go on with their argument, or conversation, or whatever it was, and she's going to hear him preach on Sunday."

"Do you feel she would wish Lady Conroy to know that she's a friend of the Rev. Byrne Fraser?" asked Bruce.

"Oh, I think so; or I wouldn't have said it."

Edith was really growing more and more loyal in her friendship. There certainly was something about Madame Frabelle that everybody, clever and stupid alike, seemed to be attracted by.

Later Edith received a telephone call from Landi. He told her that he had seen Aylmer, who was going on well, that he had begged to see her, and had been allowed by his doctor and nurse to receive a visit from her on Saturday next. He said that Aylmer had been agitated because his boy was going almost immediately to the front. He seemed very pleased at the idea of seeing her again.

Edith looked forward with a certain excitement to Saturday.

A DAY OR TWO LATER Edith received a letter from Lady Conroy, saying:

> MY DEAR EDITH,
>
> Thank you so much for your nice letter. I remember now, of course, Madame Frabelle was a friend of the Mitchells, whom I know so well, and like so much. What dears they are! Please remember me to them. I knew that she had a friend who was a clergyman, but I wasn't quite sure who it was. I suppose it must have been this Mr. Fraser. She was a Miss Pollard, you know, a very good family, and, as I always understood, the more one knows of her the better one likes her.
>
> "Thanks again for your note. I am longing to see you, and shall call directly I come to London.
>
> Ever yours,
KATHLEEN CONROY
>
> "P.S.—Madame F's husband was a French wine merchant, and a very charming man, I believe. By the way, also, she knows the Conistons, I believe, and no doubt several people we both know. Miss Clay has gone to London with one of her patients."

Bruce didn't understand why Edith was so much amused by this letter, nor why she said that she should soon write and ask Lady Conroy who Madame Frabelle was, and that she would probably answer that she was a great friend of Edith's and of the Mitchells, and the Rev. Byrne Fraser.

"She seems a little doubtful about Fraser, doesn't she?" Bruce said.

"I mean Lady Conroy. Certainly she's got rather a funny memory; she doesn't seem to have the slightest idea that she sent her to you with a letter of introduction. Now we've taken all the responsibility on ourselves."

"Well, really I don't mind," said Edith. "What does it matter? There's obviously no harm in Madame Frabelle, and never could have been."

"She's a very clever woman," said Bruce. "I'm always interested when I hear what she has to say about people. I don't mind telling you that I'm nearly always guided by it."

"So am I," said Edith.

Indeed Edith did sincerely regard her opinion as very valuable. She found her so invariably wrong that she was quite a useful guide. She was never quite sure of her own judgement until Madame Frabelle had contradicted it.

WHEN EDITH WENT TO CALL on Aylmer in the little brown house in Jermyn Street, she was shown first into the dining-room.

In a few minutes a young girl dressed as a nurse came in to speak to her.

She seemed very shy and spoke in a soft voice.

"I'm Miss Clay," she said. "I've been nursing for the last six months, but I'm not very strong and was afraid I would have to give it up when I met Mr. Ross at Boulogne. He was getting on so well that I came back to look after him and I shall stay until he is quite well, I think."

Evidently this was the Dulcie Clay Lady Conroy had mentioned. Edith was much struck by her. She was a really beautiful girl, with but one slight defect, which some people perhaps, would have rather admired—her skin was rather too dark, and a curious contrast to her beautiful blue eyes. As a rule the combination of blue eyes and dark hair goes with a fair complexion. Dulcie Clay had a brown skin, clear and pale, such as usually goes with the Spanish type of brunette. But for this curious darkness, which showed up her dazzling white teeth, she was quite lovely. It was a sweet, sensitive face, and her blue eyes, with long eyelashes like little feathers, were charming in their soft expression. Her smile was very sweet, though she had a look of melancholy. There was something touching about her.

She was below the usual height, slight and graceful. Her hair, parted in the middle, was arranged in the Madonna style in two thick natural waves each side of her face.

She had none of the bustling self-confidence of the lady nurse, but was very gentle and diffident. Surely Aylmer must be in love with her, thought Edith.

Then Miss Clay said, in her low voice:

"You are Mrs. Ottley, aren't you? I knew you at once."

"Did you? How was that?"

A little colour came into the pale, dark face.

"Mr. Ross has a little photograph of you," she said, "and once when he was very ill he gave me your name and address and asked me to send it to you if anything happened."

As she said that her eyes filled with tears.

"Oh, but he'll be all right now, won't he?" asked Edith, with a feeling of sympathy for Miss Clay, and a desire to cheer the girl.

"Yes, I think he'll be all right now," she said. "Do come up."

X

I t was a curious thing about Madame Frabelle that, though she was perfectly at ease in any society, and really had seen a good deal of the world, all her notions of life were taken from the stage. She looked upon existence from the theatrical point of view. Everyone was to her a hero or a heroine, a villain or a victim. To her a death was a *dénouement*; a marriage a happy ending. Had she known the exact circumstances in which Edith went to see the wounded hero, Madame Frabelle's dramatic remarks, the obvious observations which she would have showered on her friend, would have been quite unendurable. Therefore Edith chose to say merely that she was going to see an old friend, so as not to excite her friend's irritable imagination by any hint of sentiment or romance on the subject.

During her absence in the afternoon, it happened that Mrs. Mitchell had called, with a lady whom she had known intimately since Tuesday, so she was quite an old friend. Madame Frabelle had received them together in Edith's place. On her return Madame Frabelle was full of the stranger. She had, it seemed been dressed in bright violet, and did nothing but laugh. Whether it was that everything amused her, or merely that laughter was the only mode she knew of expressing all her sentiments, impressions and feelings, Madame Frabelle was not quite sure. Her name was Miss Radford, and she was thirty-eight. She had very red cheeks, and curly black hair. She had screamed with laughter from disappointment at hearing Mrs. Ottley was out; and shrieked at hearing that Madame Frabelle had been deputed to receive them in her place. Mrs. Mitchell had whispered that she was a most interesting person, and Madame Frabelle thought she certainly was. It appeared that Mrs. Mitchell had sent the motor somewhere during their visit, and by some mistake it was a long time coming back. This had caused peals of laughter from Miss Radford, and just as they had made up their minds to walk home the motor arrived, so she went away with Mrs. Mitchell, giggling so much she could hardly stand.

Miss Radford also had been highly amused by the charming way the boudoir was furnished, and had laughed most heartily at the curtains and the pictures. Edith was sorry to have missed her. She was evidently a valuable discovery, one of their new treasures, a rare *trouvaille* of the Mitchells.

Madame Frabelle then told Edith and Bruce that she had promised to dine with the Mitchells one day next week. Edith was pleased to find that Eglantine, and also Bruce, who had by now returned home, were so full of Mrs. Mitchell's visit and invitation, that neither of them asked her a single question about Aylmer, and appeared to have completely forgotten all about him.

As Madame Frabelle left them for a moment, Edith observed a cloud of gloom over Bruce's expressive countenance. He said:

"Well, really! Upon my word! This is a bit too much! Mind you, I'm not at all surprised. In fact, I always expected it. But it is a bit of a shock, isn't it, when you find old friends throwing you over like this?"

He walked up and down, much agitated, repeating the same thing in different words: that he had never been so surprised in his life; that it was what he had always known would happen; that it was a great shock, and he had always expected it.

At last Edith said: "I don't see anything so strange about it, Bruce. It's natural enough they should have asked her."

"Oh, is it? How would they ever have known her but for us?"

"How could they ask her without knowing her? Besides we went there last. We lunched with them only the other day."

"That's not the point. You have missed the point entirely. Unfortunately, you generally do. You have, in the most marked way, a woman's weakness, Edith. You're incapable of arguing logically. I consider it a downright slight; no, not so much a slight as an insult—perhaps injury is the *mot juste*—to take away our guest and not ask us. Not that I should have gone. I shouldn't have dreamed of going, in any case. For one thing we were there last; we lunched there only the other day. Besides, we're engaged to dine with my mother."

"Mrs. Mitchell knew that; that's why she asked Madame Frabelle because she would be alone."

"Oh, how like you, Edith! Always miss the point—always stick up for everyone but me! You invariably take the other side. However, perhaps it is all for the best; it's just as well. Nothing would have induced me to have gone—even if I hadn't been engaged, I mean. I'm getting a bit tired of the Mitchells; sick of them. Their tone is frivolous. And if they'd pressed me ever so much, nothing in the world would have made me break my promise to my mother."

"Well, then, it's all right. Why complain?"

Bruce continued, however, in deep depression till they received a message from the Mitchells, asking Edith if she and her husband couldn't manage to come, all the same, if they were not afraid of offending the elder Mrs. Ottley. They could go to Bruce's mother at any time, and the Mitchells particularly wanted them to meet some people tomorrow night—a small party, unexpectedly got up.

"Of course you won't go," said Edith to Bruce from the telephone. "You said you wouldn't under any circumstances. I'll refuse, shall I?"

"No—no, don't! Certainly not! Of course I shall go. Accept immediately. They're quite right, it is perfectly true we can go to my mother any other day. Besides, I don't think it's quite fair to old friends like the Mitchells to throw them over when they particularly want us and ask us as a special favour to them, like this."

"You don't think, perhaps, that somebody else has disappointed them, and they asked us at the last minute, to fill up?" suggested Edith, to whom this was perfectly obvious.

Bruce was furious at this suggestion.

"Certainly not!" he exclaimed. "The idea of such a thing. As if they would treat me like that! Decidedly we will go."

"All right," she said, "just as you wish. But your mother will be disappointed."

Bruce insisted. Of course the invitation was accepted, and once again he was happy!

AND AT LAST EDITH WAS able to be alone, and to think over her meeting with Aylmer. A dramatic meeting under romantic circumstances between two people of the Anglo-Saxon race always appears to fall a little flat; words are difficult to find. When she went in, to find him looking thin and weak, pale under his sunburn, changed and worn, she was deeply thrilled and touched. It brought close to her the simple, heroic manner in which so many men are calmly risking their lives, taking it as a matter of course, and as she knew for a fact that he was forty-two and had gone into the New Army at the very beginning of the war, she was aware he must have strained a point in order to join. She admired him for it.

He greeted her with that bright expression in his eyes and with the smile that she had always liked so much, which lighted up like a ray of sunshine the lean, brown, somewhat hard, face.

She sat down by his side, and all she could think of to say was: "Well, Aylmer?"

He answered: "Well, Edith! Here you are."

He took her hand, and she left it in his. Then they sat in silence, occasionally broken by an obvious remark.

WHEN HE HAD LEFT THREE years ago both had parted in love, and Aylmer in anger. He had meant never to see her again, never to forgive her for her refusal to use Bruce's escapade as a means of freeing herself, to marry him. Yet now, when they met they spoke the merest commonplaces. And afterwards neither of them could ever remember what had passed between them during the visit. She knew it was short, and that it had left an impression that calmed her. Somehow she had thought of him so much that when she actually saw him again her affection seemed cooler. Had she worn out the passion by dint of constancy? That must be strange. Unaccountably, touched as she was at his wishing to see her just after he had nearly died, the feeling now seemed to be more like a warm friendship, and less like love.

The little nurse had seen her out. Edith saw that she had been crying. Evidently she was quite devoted to Aylmer, and, poor girl, she probably regarded Edith as a rival. But Edith would not be one, of that she was determined. She wondered whether their meeting had had the same effect on Aylmer. She thought he had shown more emotion than she had.

"He will be better now," Dulcie Clay had said to her at the door. "Please come again, Mrs. Ottley."

Edith thought that generous.

It seemed to her that Dulcie was as frank and open as a child. Edith, at any rate, could read her like a book. It made her feel sorry for the girl. As Edith analysed her own feelings she wondered why she had felt no jealousy of her—only gratitude for her goodness to Aylmer.

All her sensations were confused. Only one resolution was firm in her mind. Whether he wished it or not, they should never be on the terms they were before. It could only lead to the same ending—to unhappiness. No; after all these years of separation, Edith would be his friend, and only his friend. Of that she was resolved.

XI

Lady Conroy," said Bruce thoughtfully, at breakfast next day, "is a very strict Roman Catholic."

Bruce was addicted to volunteering information, and making unanswerable remarks.

Madame Frabelle said to Edith in a low, earnest tone:

"Pass me the butter, dear," and looked attentively at Bruce.

"I sometimes think I shouldn't mind being one myself," Bruce continued; "I should rather like to eat fish on Fridays."

"But you like eating fish on Thursdays," said Edith.

"And Mr. Ottley never seems to care very much for meat."

"Unless it's particularly well cooked—in a particular way," said Edith.

"Fasts," said Madame Frabelle rather pompously, "are meant for people who like feasts."

"How true!" He gave her an admiring glance.

"I should not mind confessing, either," continued Bruce, "I think I should rather like it."

(He thought he was having a religious discussion.)

"But you always do confess," said Edith, "not to priests, perhaps, but to friends; to acquaintances, at clubs, to girls you take in to dinner. You don't call it confessing, you call it telling them a curious thing that you happen to remember."

"He calls it conversing," said Madame Frabelle. She then gave a slight flippant giggle, afterwards correcting it by a thoughtful sigh.

"The Rev. Byrne Fraser, of course, is very High Church," Bruce said. "I understood he was Anglican. By the way, was Aylmer Ross a Roman Catholic?"

"I think he is."

Bruce having mentioned his name, Edith now told him the news about her visit to their friend. Bruce liked good news—more, perhaps, because it was news than because it was good—yet the incident seemed to put him in a rather bad temper. He was sorry for Aylmer's illness, glad he was better, proud of knowing him, or, indeed, of knowing anyone who had been publicly mentioned; and jealous of the admiration visible in both Edith and Madame Frabelle. This medley of feeling resulted in his taking up a book and saying:

"Good heavens! Again I've found you've dog's-eared my book, Edith!"

"I only turned down a page," she said gently.

"No, you haven't; you've dog's-eared it. It's frightfully irritating, dear, how you take no notice of my rebukes or my comments. Upon my word, what I say to you seems to go in at one ear and out at the other, just like water on a duck's back."

"How does the water on a duck's back get into the dog's ears?—I mean the duck's ears. Oh, I'm sorry. I won't do it again."

Bruce sighed, flattened out the folded page and left the room with quiet dignity, but caught his foot in the mat. Both ladies ignored the accident.

When he had gone, Madame Frabelle said:

"Poor Edith!"

"Bruce is only a little tidy," said Edith.

"I know. My husband was dreadfully untidy, which is much worse."

"I suppose they have their faults."

"Oh, men are all alike!" exclaimed Madame Frabelle cynically.

"Only some men," said Edith. "Besides, to a woman—I mean, a nice woman—there is no such thing as men. There is a man; and either she is so fond of him that she can talk of nothing else, however unfavourably, or so much in love with him that she never mentions his name."

"Men often say women are all alike," said Madame Frabelle.

"When a man says that, he means there is only one woman in the world, and he's in love with her, and she is not in love with him."

"Men are not so faithful as women," remarked Madame Frabelle, with the air of a discovery.

"Perhaps not. And yet—well, I think the difference is that a man is often more in love with the woman he is unfaithful to than with the woman he is unfaithful with. With us it is different. . . Madame Frabelle, I think I'll take Archie with me today to see Aylmer Ross. Tell Bruce so, casually; and will you come with me another day?"

"With the greatest pleasure," said Madame Frabelle darkly, and with an expressive look. (Neither she nor Edith had any idea what it expressed.)

Edith found Aylmer wonderfully better. The pretty little nurse with the dark face and pale blue eyes told her he had had a peaceful night and had bucked up tremendously. He was seated in an arm-chair with one leg on another chair, and with him was Arthur Coniston, a great admirer of his.

It was characteristic of Aylmer, the moment he was able, to see as many friends as he was allowed. Aylmer was a very gregarious person, though—or perhaps because—he detested parties. He liked company, but hated society. Arthur Coniston, who always did his best to attract attention by his modest, self-effacing manner, was sitting with his handsome young head quite on one side from intense respect for his host, whom he regarded with the greatest admiration as a man of culture, and a judge of art. He rejoiced to be one of the first to see him, just returned after three years' absence from England, and having spent the last three months at the front.

Arthur Coniston (also in khaki), who was a born interviewer, was anxious to know Aylmer's impression of certain things over here, after his long absence.

"I should so very much like to know," he said, "what your view is of the attitude to life of the Post-Impressionists."

Aylmer smiled. He said: "I think their attitude to life, as you call it, is best expressed in some of Lear's Nonsense Rhymes: '*His Aunt Jobiska said, "Everyone knows that a pobble is better without his toes."*'"

Archie looked up in smiling recognition of these lines, and Edith laughed.

"Excuse me, but I don't quite follow you," said young Coniston gravely.

"Why, don't you see? Of course, Lear is the spirit they express. A portrait by a post-Impressionist is sure to be 'A Dong with a luminous nose.' And don't you remember, '*The owl and the pussycat went to sea in a beautiful pea-green boat*'? Wouldn't a boat painted by a Post-Impressionist be pea-green?"

"Perfectly. I see that. But—why the pobble without its toes?"

"Why, the sculptor always surrenders colour, and the painted form. Each has to give up something for the limitation of art. But the more modern artist gives up much more—likeness, beauty, a few features here and there—a limb now and then."

"Ah yes. I quite see what you mean. Like the statuary of Rodin or Epstein. One sees really only half the form, as if growing out of the sketchy sculpture. And then there's another thing—I hope I'm not wearying you?"

"No, indeed. It's great fun: such a change to hear about this sort of thing again."

"The Futurists?" asked Arthur. "What is your view of them?"

"Well, of course, they are already past, They always were. But I should say their attitude to life is that of the man who is looking at the moon reflected in a lake, but can't see it; he sees the reflection of a coal-scuttle instead."

"Ah yes. They see things wrong, you mean. They're not so real, not so logical, as the Post-Impressionists."

"Yes, the Futurist is off the rails entirely, and he seems to see hardly anything but railways. But all that noisy nonsense of the Futurists always bored me frightfully," Aylmer said. "Affectation for affectation, I prefer the pose of depression and pessimism to that of bullying and high spirits. When the affected young poet pretended to be used up and worn out, one knew there was vitality under it all. But when I see a cheerful young man shrieking about how full of life he is, banging on a drum, and blowing on a tin trumpet, and speaking of his good spirits, it depresses me, since naturally it gives the contrary impression. It can't be real. It ought to be but it isn't. If the noisy person meant what he said, he wouldn't say it."

"I see. The modern *poseurs* aren't so good as the old ones. Odle is not so clever as Beardsley."

"Of course not. Beardsley had the gift of line—though he didn't always know where to draw it—but his illustrations to Wilde's work were unsuitable, because Beardsley wanted everything down in black and white, and Wilde wanted everything in purple and gold. But both had their restraints, and their pose was reserve, not flamboyance."

"I think you mean that if people are so sickening as to have an affectation at all, you would rather they kept it quiet," said Edith.

"Exactly! At least, it brings a smile to one's lips to see a very young man pretend he is bored with life. I have often wondered what the answer would be from one of these chaps, and what he would actually say, if you held a loaded pistol to his head—I mean the man who says he doesn't think life worth living."

"What do you think he would say?" asked Coniston.

"He would scream: 'Good heavens! What are you doing? Put that down!'" said Edith.

"She's right," said Aylmer. "She always is."

Dulcie came in and brought tea.

"I hope we're not tiring him," Edith asked her.

"Oh no. I think it does him good. He enjoys it."

She sat down with Archie and talked to him gently in the corner.

"After living so much among real things," Coniston was saying, "one feels half ashamed to discuss our old subjects."

However, he and Aylmer continued to talk over books and pictures, Coniston hanging on his lips as though afraid of missing or forgetting a word he said.

Presently Edith told Aylmer about their new friend, Madame Frabelle. He was very curious to see her.

"What is she like?" he asked. "I can't imagine her living with you. Is she a skeleton at the feast?"

"A skeleton!" exclaimed Coniston. "Good heavens—no! Quite the contrary."

"A skeleton who was always feasting would hardly remain one long," suggested Edith.

"Anyhow," said Aylmer, "the cupboard is the proper place for a skeleton."

Archie had joined the group round Aylmer. Edith sat in a corner for some time, chatting with Dulcie. They arranged that Bruce was to call the next day, and Edith and Madame Frabelle the day after.

When they went away Archie, who had listened very closely to the conversation, said:

"What a lot of manners Mr. Coniston has! What did he mean by saying that Spanish painters painted a man in a gramophone?"

Edith racked her brain to remember the sentence. Then she said, with a laugh:

"Oh yes, I know! Mr. Coniston said: 'The Spanish artists painted—to a man—in monochrome.' I can't explain it, Archie. It doesn't matter. Why did you leave Miss Clay and come back to us?"

"Why, I like her all right, but you get tired of talking to women. I get bored with Dilly sometimes."

"Then you're looking forward to going back to school?"

"I shall like the society of boys of my own sex again," he said grandly.

"You're not always very nice to Dilly, Archie. I've noticed when anything is given to her, you always snatch at it. You must remember Ladies first."

"Yes, that's all very well. But then Dilly takes it all, and only gives me what's left."

Archie looked solemn.

XII

E dith," said Bruce, next morning, with some importance of manner, "I've had a letter from Aylmer—Aylmer Ross, you know—asking me, *most* particularly, to call on him."

"Oh, really," said Edith, who knew it already, as she had asked him to write to Bruce.

"He wants me to come at half-past four," said Bruce, looking over the letter pompously. "Four-thirty, to the minute. I shall certainly do it. I shan't lose a minute."

"I'm afraid you'll have to lose a few minutes," said Edith. "It's only ten o'clock."

Bruce stared at her, folded up the letter, and put it in his pocket. He thought it would be a suitable punishment for her not to see it.

Obviously he was not in the best of humours. Not being sure what was wrong, Edith adopted the simple plan of asking what he meant.

"What do I mean!" exclaimed Bruce, who, when his grievances, were vague, relied on such echoes for his most cutting effects. "You ask me what I mean? Mean, indeed!" He took some toast and repeated bitterly: "Ah! You may well ask me what I mean!"

"May I? Well, what were the observations you didn't approve of?"

"Why. . . what you said. About several minutes being lost before half-past four."

"Oh, Bruce dear, I didn't mean any harm by it."

"Harm, indeed!" repeated Bruce. "Harm! It isn't a question of actual harm. I don't say that you meant to injure me, nor even, perhaps, to hurt my feelings. But it's a way of speaking—a tone—that I think extremely *déplacé*, from you to me. Do you follow me, Edith? From *you* to *me*."

"That's a dark saying. Well, whatever I said I take it back, if you don't like it. Will that do?"

Bruce was mollified, but wouldn't show it at once.

"Ah," he said, "that's all very well. These sort of things are not so easily taken back. You should think before you speak. Prevention is better than cure."

"Yes, and a stitch in time saves nine—though it doesn't rhyme. And it's no good crying over spilt milk, and two heads are better than one. But, really, Bruce, I didn't mean it."

"What didn't you mean?"

"Good heavens, I really don't know by now! I'm afraid I've utterly forgotten what we were talking about," said Edith, looking at the door with some anxiety.

She was hoping that Madame Frabelle would soon come down and cause a diversion.

"Look here, Edith," said Bruce, "when an old friend, an old friend of yours and mine, and at one time a very intimate friend—next door to a brother—when such a friend as that has been wounded at the front, fighting for our country—and, mind you, he behaved with remarkable gallantry, for it wasn't really necessary for him to go, as he was beyond the age—well, when a friend does a thing like that, and comes back wounded, and writes, with his own hand, asking me to go and see him—well, I think it's the least I can do! I don't know what *you* think. It seems to *me* the right thing. If you disagree with me I'm very sorry. But, frankly, it appears to me that I ought to go."

"Who could doubt it?"

"Read the letter for yourself," said Bruce, suddenly taking it out of his pocket and giving it to her. "There, you see. 'Dear Ottley,' he says."

Here Bruce went to her side of the table and leant over her, reading the letter aloud to her over her shoulder, while she was reading it to herself.

"Dear Ottley,
      If you could look in tomorrow about half-past four, I
  should be very glad to see you.

                                        Yours sincerely,
                                        Aylmer Ross

Fairly cordial, I think, isn't it? Or not? Perhaps you think it cold. Would you call it a formal letter?"

Bruce took the letter out of her hand and read it over again to himself.

"Very nice, dear," said Edith.

"So I thought." He put it away with a triumphant air.

Edith was thinking that the writing was growing stronger. Aylmer must be better.

"I say, I hope it isn't a sign he's not so well, that he wants to see me. I don't call it a good sign. He's depressed. He thinks I'll cheer him up."

"And I'm sure you will. Ah, here's Madame Frabelle."

"I'm afraid I'm a little late," said their guest, with her amiable smile.

"Oh dear, no—not at all, not at all," said Bruce, who was really much annoyed at her unpunctuality. "Of course, if you'd been a minute later I shouldn't have had the pleasure of seeing you at all before I went to the office—that's all. And what does that matter? Good heavens, *that's* of no importance! Good gracious, this is Liberty Hall, I hope—isn't it? I should be very sorry for my guests to feel tied in any way—bound to be down at any particular time. Will you have some coffee? Edith, give Madame Frabelle a cup of coffee. Late? Oh dear, no; certainly not!" He gave a short, ironical laugh.

"Well, I think I'm generally fairly punctual," said Madame Frabelle, beginning her breakfast without appearing to feel this sarcasm. "What made me late this morning was that Archie and Dilly came into my room and asked me to settle a kind of dispute they were having."

"They regard you quite as a magistrate," said Edith. "But it was too bad of them to come and bother you so early."

"Oh no. Not at all. I assure you I enjoy it. And, besides, a boy with Archie's musical talents is bound to have the artistic temperament, you know, and—well—of course, we all know what that leads to—excitement; and finally a quarrel sometimes."

"If he were really musical I should have thought he ought to be more harmonious," Edith said.

"Oh, by the way, Edith, did you consult Landi about him?" Bruce inquired. "You said you intended to."

"Oh yes, I did. Landi can see no sign of musical genius yet."

"Dear, dear!" said Bruce.

"Ah, but I am convinced he's wrong. Wait a few years and you'll find he'll agree with me yet," said Madame Frabelle. "I'm not at all sure, either, that a composer like Landi is necessarily the right person to judge of youthful genius."

"Perhaps not. And yet you'd think he'd know a bit about it, too! I mean to say, they wouldn't have made him a baronet if he didn't understand his profession. Excuse my saying so, won't you?"

"Not at all," she answered. "It doesn't follow. I mean it doesn't follow that he's right about Archie. Did he try the boy's voice?" she asked Edith.

"Very much."

"How?"

"Well, he asked Archie to sing a few notes."

"And did he?"

"Yes, he did. But they weren't the notes Landi asked him to sing."

"Oh!"

"Then Landi played him two tunes, and found he didn't know one from the other."

"Well, what of that?"

"Nothing at all. Except that it showed he had no ear, as well as no voice. That is all."

Madame Frabelle would never own she was beaten.

"Ah, well, well," she said, shaking her head in an oracular way. "You wait!"

"Certainly. I shall."

"By the way, I may be a little late for dinner tonight. I'm going to see an old friend who's been wounded in the war," Bruce told Madame Frabelle proudly.

It had always been something of an ordeal to Edith when she knew that Aylmer and Bruce were alone together. It was a curious feeling, combined of loyalty to Bruce (she hated him to make himself ridiculous), loyalty to Aylmer, and an indescribable sense of being lowered in her own eyes. When they seemed friendly together it pained her self-respect. Most women will understand the sensation. However, she knew it had to be, and would be glad when it was over.

XIII

The next evening Bruce came in, holding himself very straight, with a slightly military manner. When he saw his wife he just stopped himself from saluting.

"That's a man!" he exclaimed. "That's a splendid fellow."

Edith didn't answer.

"You don't appreciate him. In my opinion Aylmer Ross is a hero."

"I hope he's better?"

"Better! He would say so, anyhow. Ah, he's a wonderful chap!" Bruce hummed Tipperary below his breath.

Edith was surprised to find herself suffering no less mental discomfort and irritation while Bruce talked about Aylmer and praised him than she used to feel years ago. It seemed as if three years had passed and altered nothing. She answered coldly. Bruce became more enthusiastic. He declared that she didn't know how to value such a fine character. "Women," he repeated, "don't know a hero when they see one."

Evidently if Bruce had had his way Aylmer would have been covered with DSO's and VC's; nothing was good enough for him.

On the other hand, if Edith had praised Aylmer, Bruce would have been the first to *debiner* his actions, undervalue his gifts, and crab him generally.

Edith was not one of those women, far more common than is supposed, who consider themselves aggrieved and injured when a discarded lover consoles himself with someone else. Nor was she one of the numerous people who will not throw away what they no longer want for fear someone else will pick it up. She had such a strong sympathy for Dulcie Clay that she had said to herself several times she would like to see her perfectly happy. Edith was convinced that the nurse adored her patient, but she was not at all sure that he returned the admiration. Edith herself had only seen him alone once, and on that occasion they had said hardly anything to each other. He had been constrained and she had been embarrassed. The day that Arthur Coniston was there and they talked of pictures, Aylmer had given her, by a look, to understand that he would like to see her again alone, and she knew perfectly well, even without that, that he was longing for another *tête-à-tête*.

However, the next day Edith went with Madame Frabelle.

This was a strangely unsatisfactory visit. Edith knew his looks and every tone of his voice so well that she could see that Aylmer, unlike everybody else, was not in the least charmed with Madame Frabelle. She bored him; he saw nothing in her.

Madame Frabelle was still more disappointed. She had been told he was brilliant; he said nothing put commonplaces. He was supposed to be witty; he answered everything she said literally. He was said to be a man of encyclopaedic information; but when Madame Frabelle questioned him on such subjects his answers were dry and short; and when she tried to draw him out about the war, he changed the subject in a manner that was not very far from being positively rude.

Leaving them for a moment, Edith went to talk to Dulcie.

"How do you think he's getting on?" she said.

"He's getting well; gradually. He seems a little nervous the last day or so."

"Do you think he's been seeing too many people?"

"He hasn't seen more than the doctor has allowed. But, do you know, Mrs. Ottley, I think it depends a great deal who the people are."

She waited a moment and then went on in a low voice:

"You do him more good than anyone. You see, he's known you so long," she added gently, "and so intimately. It's no strain—I mean he hasn't got to make conversation."

"Yes, I see," said Edith.

"Mr. Ross hasn't any near relations—no mother or sister. You seem to take their place—if you understand what I mean."

Edith thought it charmingly tactful of her to put it like that.

"I'm sure *you* take their place," Edith said.

Dulcie looked down.

"Oh, of course, he hasn't to make any effort with me. But then *I* don't amuse him, and he wants amusement, and change. It's a great bore for a man like that—so active mentally, and in every way—to have to lie perfectly still, especially when he has no companion but me. I'm rather dull in some ways. Besides, I don't know anything about the subjects he's interested in."

"Don't talk nonsense," said Edith, smiling. "I should imagine that just to look at you would be sufficient."

"Oh, Mrs. Ottley! How can you?"

She turned away as if rather pained than pleased at the compliment.

"I haven't very high spirits," she said. "I'm not sure that I don't sometimes depress him."

ADA LEVERSON

"On the contrary; I'm sure he wouldn't like a breezy, restless person bouncing about the room and roaring with laughter," Edith said.

She smiled. "Perhaps not. But there might be something between. He will be able to go for a drive in a week or two. I wondered whether, perhaps, you could take him out?"

"Oh yes; I dare say that could be arranged."

"I have to go out all tomorrow afternoon. I wondered whether you would come and sit with him, Mrs. Ottley?"

"Certainly I will, if you like."

"Oh, please do! I know he's worrying much more about his son than anybody thinks. You see, the boy's really very young, and I'm not sure he's strong."

"I suppose neither of them told the truth about their age," said Edith. "It reminds one of the joke in *Punch*: 'Where do you expect to go if you tell lies? To the front.'"

Miss Clay gave a little laugh. Then she started. A bell was heard ringing rather loudly.

"I'll tell him you're coming tomorrow, then," she said.

They returned to Aylmer's room.

He was looking a little sulky. He said as Edith came in:

"I thought you'd gone without saying good-bye. What on earth were you doing?"

"Only talking to Miss Clay," said Edith, sitting down by him. "How sweet she is."

"Charming," said Madame Frabelle. "Wonderfully pretty, too."

"She's a good nurse," said Aylmer briefly. "She's been awfully good to me. But I do hope I shan't need her much longer." He spoke with unnecessary fervour.

"Oh, Mr. Ross!" exclaimed Madame Frabelle. "I'm sure if I were a young man I should be very sorry when she had to leave me!"

"Possibly. However, you're not a young man. Neither am I."

There was a moment's silence. This was really an exceptional thing when Madame Frabelle was present. Edith could not recall one occasion when Eglantine had had nothing to say. Aylmer must have been excessively snubbing. Extraordinary I Wonder of wonders! He had actually silenced Madame Frabelle!

All Aylmer's natural politeness and amiability returned when they rose to take their leave. He suddenly became cordial, cheery and charming. Evidently he was so delighted the visitor was going that it quite raised his spirits. When they left he gave Edith a little reproachful look. He did not ask her to come again. He was afraid she would bring Madame Frabelle.

"Well, Edith, I thoroughly understand your husband's hero-worship for that man," said Madame Frabelle (meaning she thoroughly misunderstood it). "I've been studying his character all this afternoon."

"Do tell me what you think of him!"

"Edith, I'm sorry to say it, but it's a hard, cold, cruel nature."

"Is it really?"

"Mr. Aylmer Ross doesn't know what it is to feel emotion, sentiment, or tenderness. Principle he has, perhaps, and no doubt he thinks he has great self-control, but that's only because he's absolutely incapable of passion of any kind."

Edith smiled.

"I see you're amused at my being right again. It is an odd thing about me, I must own. I never make a mistake," said Madame Frabelle complacently.

As they walked home, she continued to discourse eloquently on the subject of Aylmer. She explained him almost entirely away.

There was nothing Madame Frabelle fancied herself more on than physiognomy. She pointed out to Edith how the brow showed a narrow mind, the mouth bitterness. (How extraordinarily bored Aylmer must have been to give that impression of all others, thought her listener.) And the eyes, particularly, gave away his chief characteristic, the thing that one missed most in his personality.

"And what is that?"

"Can't you see?"

"No, I don't think I can."

"He has no sense of humour!" said Madame Frabelle triumphantly.

After a few moment's pause, Edith said:

"What do you think of Miss Clay?"

"She's very pretty—extremely pretty. But I don't quite like to say what I think of her. I'd rather not. Don't ask me. It doesn't concern me."

"As bad as that? Oh, do tell me. You're so interesting about character, Eglantine."

"Dear Edith, how kind of you. Well, she's very, very clever, of course. Most intellectual. A remarkable brain, I should say. But she's deep and scheming; it's a sly, treacherous face."

"Really, I can't see that."

Madame Frabelle put her hand on Edith's shoulder. They had just reached the house.

"Ah, you don't know so much of life as I do, my dear."

"I should have said she is certainly not at all above the average in cleverness, and I think her particularly simple and frank."

"Ah, but that's all put on. You'll see I'm right some day. However, it doesn't matter. No doubt she's a very good nurse."

"Don't abuse her to Bruce," said Edith, as they went in.

"Certainly not. But why do you mind?"

"I don't know; I suppose I like her."

Madame Frabelle laughed. "How strange you are!"

She lowered her voice as they walked upstairs, and said:

"To tell the real truth, she gave me a shiver down the spine. I believe that girl capable of anything. That dark skin with those pale blue eyes! I strongly suspect she has a touch of the tarbrush."

"My dear! Nonsense. You can't have looked at her fine little features and her white hands."

"Why is she so dark?"

"There may have been Italian or Spanish blood in her family," said Edith, laughing. "It's not a symptom of crime."

"There may, indeed," replied Madame Frabelle in a tone of deep meaning, as they reached the door of her room. "But, mark my words, Edith, that's a dangerous woman!"

AN EVENT HAD OCCURRED IN the Ottley household during their absence. Archie had brought home a dog and implored his mother to let him keep it.

"What sort of dog is it?" asked Edith.

"Come and look at it. It isn't any particular *sort*. It's just a dog."

"But, my dear boy, you're going to school the day after tomorrow, and you can't take it with you."

"I know; but I'll teach Dilly to look after it."

It was a queer, rough, untidy-looking creature; it seemed harmless enough; a sort of Dobbin in *Vanity Fair* in the canine world.

"It's an inconsistent dog. Its face is like a terrier's, and its tail like a sort of spaniel," said Archie. "But I think it might be trained to a bloodhound."

"You do, do you? What use would a bloodhound be to Dilly?"

"Well, you never know. It might be very useful."

"I'm afraid there's not room in the house for it."

"Oh, Mother!" both the children cried together. "We *must* keep it!"

"Was it lost?" she asked.

Archie frowned at Dilly, who was beginning to say, "Not exactly."

"Tell me how you got it."

"It was just walking along, and I took its chain. The chain was dragging on the ground."

"You stole it," said Dilly.

Archie flew at her, but Edith kept him back.

"Stole it! I didn't! Its master had walked on and evidently didn't care a bit about it, poor thing. That's not stealing."

"If Master Archie wants to keep a lot of dogs, he had better take them with him to school," said the nurse. "I don't want nothing to do with no dogs, not in this nursery."

"There's only one thing to be done, Archie; you must take care of it for the next day or two, and I shall advertise in the paper for its master."

"Oh, mother!"

"Don't you see it isn't even honest to keep it?"

Archie was bitterly disappointed, but consoled at the idea of seeing the advertisement in the paper.

"How can we advertise it? We don't know what name it answers to."

"It would certainly be difficult to describe," said Edith.

They had tried every name they had ever heard of, and Dilly declared it had answered to them all, if answering meant jumping rather wildly round them and barking as if in the very highest spirits, it certainly had.

"It'll be fun to see my name in the paper," said Archie thoughtfully.

"Indeed you won't see your name in the paper."

"Well, I found it," said Archie rather sulkily.

"Yes; but you had no right to find it, and still less to bring it home. I don't know what your father will say."

Bruce at once said that it must be taken to Scotland Yard. Dilly cried bitterly, and said she wanted it to eat out of her hand, and save her life in a snowstorm.

"It's not a St Bernard, you utter little fool," said her brother.

"Well, it might save me from drowning," said Dilly.

She had once seen a picture, which she longed to realise, of a dog swimming, holding a child in its mouth. She thought it ought to be called Faithful or Rover.

All these romantic visions had to be given up. Madame Frabelle said the only thing to do was to take it at once to the Battersea Dogs' Home, where it would be "happy with companions of its own age". Immediately after dinner her suggestion was carried out, to the great relief of most of the household. The nurse said when it had gone that she had "known all along it was mad, but didn't like to say so."

"But it took such a fancy to me," said Archie.

"Perhaps that was why," said Dilly.

THE CHILDREN WERE SEPARATED BY force.

XIV

For a woman who was warm-hearted, sensitive and thoughtful, Edith had a singularly happy disposition. First, she was good-tempered; not touchy, not easily offended about trifles. Such vanity as she had was not in an uneasy condition; she cared very little for general admiration, and had no feeling for competition. She was without ambition to be superior to others. Then, though she saw more deeply into things than the generality of women, she was not fond of dwelling on the sad side of life. Very small things pleased her, while trifles did not annoy her. Hers was not the placidity of the stupid, fat, contented person who never troubles about other people.

She was rather of a philosophical turn, and her philosophy tended to seeing the brighter side. Where she was singularly fortunate was that though she felt pleasure deeply—a temperament that feels pain in proportion—her suffering, though acute, seldom lasted long. There was an elasticity in her disposition that made her rebound quickly from a blow.

Her affections were intense, but she did not suffer the usual penalty of love—a continual dread of losing the loved object. If she adored her children and was thankful for their health and beauty, she was not exactly what is called an anxious mother. She thought much about them, and was very determined to have her own way in anything concerning them. That, indeed, was a subject on which she would give way to no-one. But as she had so far succeeded in directing them according to her own ideas, she was satisfied. And she was very hopeful. She could look forward to happiness, but troubles she dealt with as they arose.

Certainly, after the first few months of their marriage, Bruce had turned out a disappointment. But now that she knew him, knew the worst of him, she did not think bad. He had an irritating personality. But most people had to live with someone who was a little irritating; and she was so accustomed to his various ways and weaknesses that she could deal with them unmoved, almost mechanically. She did not take him seriously. She would greatly have preferred, of course, that he should understand her, that she could look up to him and lean on him. But as this was not so, she made the best of it, and managed to be contented enough. Three years ago she had not even known she could be deeply in love.

of her age, but the contour of Edith's face was still as youthful as ever; she had one of those clearly shaped oval faces that are not disposed to growing thick and broad, or to haggardness. The oval might be a shade wider than it was three years ago; that was all the more becoming; did it not make the features look smaller?

As she went out she laughed at herself for giving so much thought to her appearance. It was as though she believed she was going to play an important part in the chief scene of a play.

Once dressed, as usual she lost all self-consciousness, and thought of outside things.

Miss Clay was out, as she had told Edith she would be, and the servant showed her in.

She saw at once that Aylmer, also, had been looking forward to this moment with some excitement. He, too, had dressed with special care; and she knew, without being told, that orders had been given to receive no other visitors.

He was sitting in an arm-chair, with the bandaged leg on the other chair, a small table by his side laid for tea. Even a kettle was boiling (no doubt to avoid interruption). It was his old brown library, where she had occasionally seen him with others in the old days. But this was literally the first time she had seen him in his own house alone.

It was essentially a man's room. Comfortable, but not exactly luxurious; very little was sacrificed to decoration.

There were a few very old dark pictures on the walls. The room was crammed with books in long, low bookcases. On the mantelpiece was a pewter vase of cerise-coloured carnations.

An uncut *English Review* was in his hand, but he threw it on the floor with a characteristic gesture as she came in.

"You look very comfortable," said Edith, as she took her seat in the arm-chair placed for her.

He answered gravely, speaking in his direct, quick way, with his sincere manner:

"It was very good of you to come."

"Shall I pour out your tea?"

"Yes. Let's have tea and get it over."

She laughed, took off her gloves, and he watched her fingers as they occupied themselves with the china, as though he were impatient for the ceremony to be finished.

While she poured it out and handed it to him he said not a word. She saw that he looked pale and seemed rather nervous. Each tried to put the other at ease, more by looks than words. Edith saw it would worry him to make conversation. They knew each other well enough to exchange ideas without words.

He had something to say and she would not postpone it. That would irritate him.

"There," said Aylmer, giving a little push to the table. "Do you want any more tea?"

"No, thanks."

"Well—do you mind coming a little nearer?"

She lifted the little table, put it farther behind his chair, placed the arm-chair closer to him by the fire, and sat down again. He looked at her for some time with a serious expression. Then he said, rather abruptly and unexpectedly:

"What a jolly hat!"

"Oh, I *am* glad you like it!" exclaimed Edith. "I was afraid you'd hate it."

For the first time they were talking in their old tone, she reflected.

"No, I like it—I love it." He lowered his voice to say this.

"I'm glad," she repeated.

"And I love you," said Aylmer as abruptly, and in a still lower voice.

She didn't answer.

"Look here, Edith. I want to ask you something."

"Yes."

He seemed to have some difficulty in speaking. He was agitated.

"Have you forgotten me?"

"You can see I haven't, or I wouldn't be here," she answered.

"Don't fence with me. I mean, really. Are you the same as when I went away?"

"Aylmer, do you think we had better talk about it?"

"We must. I must. I can't endure the torture of seeing you just like anybody else. You know I told you—" He stopped a moment.

"You told me you'd never be a mere friend," she said. "But everything's so different now!"

"It isn't different; that's where you're wrong. You're just the same, and so am I. Except that I care for you far more than I ever did."

"Oh, Aylmer!"

"When I thought I was dying I showed your little photograph to

Miss Clay. I told her all about it. I suppose I was rather mad. It was just after an operation. It doesn't matter a bit; she wouldn't ever say a word."

"I'm sure she wouldn't."

"I had to confide in somebody," he went on. "I told her to send you back the photograph, and I told her that my greatest wish was to see you again."

"Well, my dear boy, we have met again! Do change your mind from what you said last! I mean when you went away." She spoke in an imploring tone.

"Do you wish to be friends, then?"

She hesitated a moment, then said: "Yes, I do."

XV

After a moment's pause he said: "You say everything's changed. In a way it is. I look at things differently—I regard them differently. When you've been up against it, and seen life and death pretty close, you realise what utter rot it is to live so much for the world."

Edith stared. "But... doesn't it make you feel all the more the importance of principle—goodness and religion, and all that sort of thing? I expected it would, with you."

"Frankly, no; it doesn't. Now, let us look at the situation quietly."

After an agitated pause he went on:

"As far as I make out, you're sacrificing yourself to Bruce. When he ran away with that girl, and begged you to divorce him, you could have done it. You cared for me. Everything would have been right, even before the world. No-one would have blamed you. Yet you wouldn't."

"But that *wasn't* for the world, Aylmer; you don't understand. It was for myself. Something in me, which I can't help. I felt Bruce needed me and would go wrong without me—"

"Why should you care? Did he consider you?"

"That isn't the point, dear boy. I felt as if he was my son, so to speak—a sort of feeling of responsibility."

"Yes, quite. It was quixotic rubbish. That's my opinion. There!"

Edith said nothing, remembering he was still ill.

"Well," he went on, "now, he *hasn't* run away from you. He's stayed with you for three years; utterly incapable of appreciating you, as I know he is, bothering you to death."

"Oh, Aylmer!"

"Don't I know him? You're wasting and frittering yourself away for nothing."

"The children—"

"Don't you think I'd have looked after the children better than he?"

"Yes, I do, Aylmer. But he *is* their father. They may keep him straight."

"I consider you're utterly wasted," he said. "Well! He's stuck to you, apparently, for these last three years (as far as you know), and now I'm going to ask you something entirely different, for the last time. When I was dying, or thought I was, things showed themselves clearly enough, I can tell you. And I made up my mind if I lived to see you, to say this. Leave Bruce, with me!"

She stared at him.

"In six weeks, when he's tired of telling his friends at the club about it, he'll make up his mind, I suppose, if you insist, or even without, to divorce you. But do you suppose he'll keep the children? No, my dear of course he won't. You'll never have to leave them. I would never ask you that. Now listen!" He put his hand over hers, not caressingly, but to keep her quiet. "He'll want to marry again, won't he?"

"Very likely," she answered.

"Probably already he's in love with that woman What's-her-name—Madame Frabelle—who's staying with you."

Edith gave a little laugh.

"Perhaps he's in love with her already," continued Aylmer.

"Quite impossible!" said Edith calmly.

"She's a very good sort. She's not a fool, like the girl. She'd look after Bruce very well."

"So she would," answered Edith.

"Bruce will adore her, be under her thumb, and keep perfectly 'straight', as you call it—as straight as he ever would. Won't he?"

She was silent.

"You'll get the children then, don't you see?"

"Yes. With a bad reputation, with a cloud on my life, to bring up Dilly!"

He sighed impatiently, and said: "You see, you don't see things as they really are, even now. How could you ever possibly hurt Dilly? You're only thinking of what the world says, now."

"Hear me out," he went on. "Is this the only country? After the war, won't everything be different? Thank goodness, I'm well provided for. You needn't take a farthing. Leave even your own income to Bruce if you like. You know I've five thousand a year now, Edith?"

"I didn't know it. But that has nothing on earth to do with it," she answered.

"Bosh! It has a great deal to do with it. I can afford to bring your children up as well as Teddy, my boy. We can marry. And in a year or two no one would think any more about it."

"You bewilder me," said Edith.

"I want to. Think it over. Don't be weak. I'm sorry, dear, to ask you to take the blame on your side. It's unfair; but after all, perhaps, it's straighter than waiting for an opportunity (which you could easily get in time) of finding Bruce in the wrong."

Her face expressed intense determination and disagreement with his views.

"Don't answer me," he said, "think—"

"My dear boy, you must let me answer you. Will you listen to me?"

"Go on, Edith. I'll always listen to you."

"You don't realise it, but you're not well," she said.

He gave an impatient gesture.

"How like a woman! As soon as I talk sense you say I'm not well. A broken leg doesn't affect the brain, remember."

"No, Aylmer; I don't mean that. But you've been thinking this over till you've lost your bearings, your sense of proportion. . ."

"Rot! I've just got it! That's what you mean. It comes to this, my dear girl"—he spoke gently. "Of course, if you don't care for me, my suggestion would be perfectly mad. Perhaps you don't. Probably you regard our romance as a pretty little story to look back on."

"No, I don't, unless—"

"I won't ask you straight out," he said. "I don't suppose you know yourself. But, if you care for me, as I do for you"—he spoke steadily—"you'll do as I ask."

"I might love you quite as much, and yet not do it."

"I know it's a big thing. It's a sacrifice, in a way. But don't you see, Edith, that if you still like me, your present life is a long, slow sacrifice to convention, or (as you say) to a morbid sense of responsibility?"

She looked away with a startled expression.

"Well, do you love me?" he said rather impatiently, but yet with his old charm of tenderness and sincerity. "I have never changed. As you know, after the operation, when they thought I was practically done in—it may seem a bit mad, but I was really more sane than I have ever been—I told Dulcie Clay all about it."

She stopped him. "I know you did, my dear, and I don't blame you a bit. She's absolutely loyal. But now, listen. Has nothing occurred to you about her?"

"Nothing, except that I'm hoping to get rid of her as soon as possible."

"She's madly in love with you, Aylmer."

He looked contemptuous.

"She's a dear girl," said Edith. "I feel quite fond of her."

"Really, I don't see how she comes in. You are perverse, Edith!"

"I'm not perverse. I see things."

"She's never shown the slightest sign of it," said Aylmer. "I think it's your imagination. But even if it's not, it isn't my business, nor yours."

"I think it is, a little."

"If you talk like that, I'll send her away today."

"Oh, Aylmer! how ungrateful of you to say such a thing! She's been an angel."

He spoke wearily. "I don't want *angels*! I want *you*!" He suddenly leant forward and took her hands.

She laughed nervously. "What a compliment."

Then she disengaged herself and stood up.

Aylmer sighed. "Now you're going to say, Ought you to talk so much? What is your temperature? Oh, women *are* irritating, even the nicest, confound them!"

Edith was unable to help laughing.

"I'm afraid I *was* going to say something like that."

"Now, are you going to say you won't answer me for fear it will excite me?"

"Don't talk nonsense," said Edith. "*I* take you seriously enough. Don't worry!"

He looked delighted.

"Thank heaven! Most women treat a wounded man as if he were a sick child or a lunatic. It's the greatest rot. I'm nearly well."

Edith looked round for his tonic, but stopped herself.

"Are you going now?" he asked.

"No, Aylmer. I thought of stopping a few minutes, if you don't mind."

"Shall we talk of something else," said Aylmer satirically, "to divert my thoughts? Hasn't it been lovely weather lately?"

She smiled and sat down again.

"Would you like to know how soon the war will be over?" he went on. "Oddly enough, I really don't know!"

"Are you going back when you've recovered?" she asked abruptly.

"Of course I'm going back; and I want to go back with your promise." Then he looked a little conscience-stricken. "Dear Edith, I don't want to rush you. Forgive me."

They both sat in dead silence for five minutes. He was looking at the black velvet toque on the fair hair, over the soft eyes. She was staring across at the cherry-coloured carnations in the pewter vase on the mantelpiece.

As has been said, they often exchanged ideas without words.

He remarked, as she glanced at a book: "Yes, I have read *A Life of Slavery*. Have you? Do you think it good?"

"Splendid," Edith answered; "it's a labour of hate."

He laughed.

"Quite true. One can't call it a labour of love, though it was written to please the writer—not the public."

"I wonder you could read it," said Edith, "after what you've been through."

"It took my thoughts off life," he said.

"Why? Isn't it life?"

"Of course it is. Literary life."

Edith looked at the clock.

"When am I going to see you again?" he asked in a rather exhausted voice.

"Whenever you like. What about taking you out for a drive next week?"

"Right."

"I'll think over what you said," said Edith casually as she stood up.

"What a funny little speech. You're *impayable*! Oh, you are a jolly girl!"

"'Jolly' girl," repeated Edith, not apparently pleased. "I'm thirty-five, with a boy at school and a growing girl of seven!"

"You think too much of the almanac. I'm forty-one, with a son at the front."

"How on earth did you get your commissions?"

"In the usual way. Teddy and I told lies. He said he was eighteen and I said I was thirty-nine."

"I see. Of course."

He rang the bell.

"Will you write to me, dear Edith?"

"No. I'll come and see you, Aylmer."

"Are you going to bring Archie, Bruce, or Madame Frabelle?"

"Neither."

"Do leave Madame Frabelle at home."

"Though you don't like her, you might pronounce her name right! She's such a clever woman."

"She's an utter fool," said Aylmer.

"Same thing, very often," said Edith. "Don't worry. Good-bye."

She went away, leaving him perfectly happy and very hungry.

HARDLY HAD SHE GONE WHEN Miss Clay came in and brought him some beef-tea on a tray.

XVI

To Edith's joy, as they entered the Mitchell's huge, familiar drawing-room, the first person she saw was her beloved confidant, Sir Tito Landi. This was the friend of all others whom she most longed to see at this particular moment.

The extraordinary confidence and friendship between the successful Italian composer and Edith Ottley needs, perhaps, a word of explanation. He was adored equally in the artistic and the social worlds, and was at once the most cynical of Don Juans and the most unworldly of Don Quixotes. He was a devoted and grateful friend, and a contemptuous but not unforgetful enemy.

It was not since his celebrity that Edith had first met him; she had known him intimately all her life. From her earliest childhood she had, so to speak, been brought up on Landi; on Landi's music and Landi's views of life. He had been her mother's music teacher soon after he first made a name in London; and long before he was the star whose singing or accompanying was a rare favour, and whose presence gave a cachet to any entertainment.

How many poor Italians—yes, and many people of other nationalities—had reason to bless his acquaintance! How kind, how warm-hearted, how foolishly extravagant on others was Landi! His brilliant cleverness, which made him received almost as an Englishman among English people, was not, however, the cleverness of the *arriviste*. Although he had succeeded, and success was his object, no one could be less self-interested, less pushing, less scheming. In many things he was a child. He would as soon dine at Pagani's with a poor sculptor, or a poor and plain woman who was struggling to give lessons in Italian, as with the most brilliant hostess in London. And he always found fashion and ceremony a bore. He was so great a favourite in England that he had been given that most English of titles, a knighthood, just as though he were very rich, or political, or a popular actor. In a childish way it amused him, and he was pleased with it. But though he was remarkable for his courtly tact, he loved most of all to be absolutely free and Bohemian, to be quite natural among really sympathetic, witty, or beautiful friends. He liked to say what he thought, to go where he wished, and to make love when he chose, not when other people chose. He had long been a man with an assured position, but he had changed little since he was twenty-one, and arrived from Naples with only his talent, his bright blue eyes, his fair complexion, his small, dignified figure and his daring humour. Yet the music he wrote indicated his sensitive and deeply feeling nature, and though his conversation could hardly be called other than cynical, nor his jokes puritanical, there was always in him a vein of genuine—not sentimental, but perhaps romantic—love and admiration for everything good; good in music, good in art, good in character. He laid down no rules of what was good. "Tout savoir c'est tout pardonner" was perhaps his motto. But he was very unexpected; that was one of his charms. He would pass over the most extraordinary things—envious slights, small injuries, things another man would never forgive. On the other hand, he retained a bitter memory, not at all without its inclination for repayment, for other trifles that many would disregard.

EVER SINCE SHE WAS A child Edith had been his special favourite. He loved the privilege of calling her Edith, of listening to her confidences, of treating her with loving familiarity. It was a joke between them that, while he used formerly to say, "Cette enfant! Je l'ai vue en jupe courte, vous savez!" he had gradually reached the point of declaring, "Je l'ai vue naître!" almost with tears in his eyes.

This explains why Landi was the only creature to whom Edith could tell everything, and did. Must not all nice people have a confidant? And no girl or woman friend—much as they might like her, and she them— could ever take the place of Landi, the wise and ever-sympathetic.

There was something in his mental attitude that was not unfeminine, direct and assertive as he was. He had what is generally known as feminine intuition, a quality perhaps even rarer in women than in men.

TONIGHT THE PERSISTENTLY HOSPITABLE MRS. MITCHELL had a large party. Dressed in grey, she was receiving her guests in the big room on the ground floor, and tactfully directing the conversation of a crowd of various and more or less interesting persons.

It was one of those parties that had been described as a Russian Salad, where one ran an equal risk—or took an equal chance—of being taken to dinner by Charlie Chaplin or Winston Churchill, and where society and the stage were equally well represented. Young officers on leave and a few pretty girls filled the vacancies.

As Bruce, Edith and Madame Frabelle came in together, Landi went straight to Edith's side.

Looking at her through his eyeglass, he said, as if to himself, in an anxious tone:

"Elle a quelquechose, cette enfant; oui, elle a quelquechose," and as the last guest had not arrived he sat down thoughtfully by her on the small sofa.

"Yes, Landi, there is something the matter. I'm longing to tell you about it. I want your advice," said Edith, smiling.

"Tout se sait; tout se fait; tout s'arrange," sententiously remarked Landi, who was not above talking oracular commonplaces at times.

"Oh, it isn't one of those things, Landi."

"Not? Are you sure? Don't be sad, Edith. Be cheerful. Tiens! Tiens! Tiens! How excited you are," he went on, as she looked at him with perfect composure.

"You will think I have reason to be excited when I tell you."

He smiled in an experienced way.

"I'll sit next to you at dinner and you shall tell me everything. Tiens! La vieille qui voit double!" He bowed politely as Madame Frabelle came up.

"Dear Sir Tito, *what* a pleasure to see you again! Your lovely songs have been ringing in my ears ever since I heard them!"

"Where did you hear them? On a piano-organ?" he asked.

"You're too bad! Isn't he naughty? No, when you sang here last."

Mr. Mitchell came up, and Madame Frabelle turned away.

"Dieu merci! La pauvre! Elle me donne sur les nerfs ce soir," said Landi. "I shall sit next to you whether the cards are placed so or not, Edith, and you'll tell me everything between the soup and the ices."

"I will indeed."

"Madame Meetchel," he said, looking round through his eyeglass, "is sure to have given you a handsome young man, someone who ought to drive Bruce wild with jealousy, but doesn't, or. . . or. . ."

"Or some fly-blown celebrity."

"Sans doute!"

The door opened and the last guest appeared. It was young Coniston (in khaki), who was invariably asked when there was to be music. He was so useful.

He approached Landi at once.

"Ah, cher maître, quel plaisir!" he said with his South Kensington accent and his Oxford manner. (He had been a Cambridge man.)

"C'est vrai?" asked Landi, who had his own way of dismissing a person in a friendly way.

Coniston began talking to him of a song. Landi waved him off and went up to Mrs. Mitchell, said something which made her laugh and blush and try to hit him with her fan—the fan, the assault and the manner were all out of date, but Mrs. Mitchell made no pretence at going with the times—and his object was gained.

SIR TITO TOOK EDITH IN to dinner.

XVII

As they found their places at the long table (Sir Tito had exchanged cards, as though he meant to fight a duel with Edith's destined partner) of course the two turned their backs to one another. On her other side was Mr. Mitchell. When Madame Frabelle noticed this, she gave Edith an arch shake of the head, and made a curious warning movement with her hand. Edith smiled at her in astonishment. She had utterly forgotten her friend's fancy about the imaginary intrigue supposed to be going on between her and Mr. Mitchell, and she wondered what the gesture meant. Sir Tito also saw it, and, turning round to Edith, said in a low voice:

"Qu'est-ce-qu'elle a, la vieille?"

"I really don't know. I never understand signs. I've forgotten the code, I suppose!"

Mr. Mitchell, after a word to the person he had taken down, gladly turned to Edith. He always complained that the host was obliged to sit between the oldest and the most boring guests. It was unusual for him to have so pretty a neighbour as Edith. But he was a collector: his joy was to see a heterogeneous mass of people, eating and laughing at his table. For his wife there were a few social people, for him the Bohemians, and always the younger guests.

"Not bad—not bad, is it?" he said, looking critically round down the two sides of the table, while his kind pink face beamed with hospitable joy.

"You've got a delightful party tonight."

"What I always say is," said Mr. Mitchell; "let them enjoy themselves! Dash it, I hate etiquette." He lowered his voice. "Bruce is looking pretty blooming. Not so many illnesses lately has he?"

"Not when he's at home," said Edith.

"Ah! At the F O the dear fellow does, I'm afraid, suffer a good deal from nerves," said Mr. Mitchell, especially towards the end of the day. About four o'clock, I mean, you know! You know old Bruce! Good sort he is. I see he hasn't got the woman I meant him to sit next to, somehow or other. I see he's next to Miss Coniston."

"Oh, he likes her."

"Good, good. Thought she was a bit too artistic, and high-browed, as the Americans say, for him. But now he's used to that sort of thing, isn't he? Madame Frabelle, eh? Wonderful woman. No soup, Edith: why not?"

"It makes me silent," said Edith; "and I like to talk."

Mitchell laughed loudly. "Ha ha! Champagne for Mrs. Ottley. What are you about?" He looked up reprovingly at the servant. Mr. Mitchell was the sort of man who never knows, after twenty years' intimate friendship, whether a person takes sugar or not.

Edith allowed the man to fill her glass. She knew it depressed Mr. Mitchell to see people drinking water. So she only did it surreptitiously, and as her glass was always full, because she never drank from it, Mr. Mitchell was happy.

A very loud feminine laugh was heard.

"That's Miss Radford," said Mr. Mitchell. "That's how she always goes on. She's always laughing. She was immensely charmed with you the day she called on you with my wife."

"Was she?" said Edith, who remembered she herself had been out on that occasion.

"Tremendously. I can't remember what she said: I think it was how clever you were."

"She saw Madame Frabelle. I wasn't at home."

"Ha ha! Good, very good!" Mr. Mitchell turned to his other neighbour.

"Eh bien," said Sir Tito, who was waiting his opportunity. "Commence!"

At once Edith began murmuring in a low voice her story of herself and Aylmer, and related today's conversation in Jermyn Street.

Sir Tito nodded his head occasionally. When he listened most intently, he appeared to be looking round the table at other people. He lifted a glass of champagne and bowed over it to Mrs. Mitchell; then he put his hand to his lips and blew a kiss.

"Who's that for?" Edith asked, interrupting herself.

"C'est pour la vieille."

"Madame Frabelle! Why do you kiss your hand to her?"

"To keep her quiet. Look at her: she's so impressed, and thinks it so wicked, that she's blushing and uncomfortable. I've a splendid way, Edith (pardon), of silencing all these elderly ladies who make love to me. I don't say 'Ferme!' I'm polite to them."

Edith laughed. Sir Tito was not offended.

"Yes, you needn't laugh, my dear child. I'm not old enough yet pour les jeunes; at any rate, if I am they don't know it. I'm still pursued by the upper middle-age class, with gratitude for favours to come (as they think)."

"Well, what's your plan?"

He giggled.

"I tell Madame Frabelle, Madame Meetchel, Lady Everard—first, that they have beautiful lips; then, that I can't look at them without longing to kiss them. Lady Everard, after I said that, kept her hand before her face the whole evening, so as not to distract me, and drive me mad. Consequently she couldn't talk."

"Do they really believe you?"

"Evidemment! . . . I wonder," he continued mischievously, as he refused wine, "whether Madame Frabelle will confess to you tonight about my passion for her, or whether she will keep it to herself?"

"I dare say she'll tell me. At least she'll ask me if I think so or not."

"Si elle te demande, tu diras que tu n'en sais rien! Well, I think. . ."

"What?"

"You must wait. Wait and see. Really, it's impossible, my dear child, for you to accept an invitation for an elopement as if it were a luncheon-party. Not only that, it's good for Aylmer to be kept in doubt. Excellent for his health."

"Really?"

"When I say his health, I mean the health and strength of his love for you. You must vacillate, Edith. Souvent femme varie. You sit on the fence, n'est-ce-pas? Well, offer the fence to him. But, take it away before he sits down. Voilà!"

Edith laughed. "But then this girl, Miss Clay, she's always there. And I like her."

"What is her nationality?"

"How funny you should ask that! I think she must be of Spanish descent. She's so quiet, so religious, and has a very dark complexion. And yet wonderful light blue eyes."

"Quelle histoire! Qu'est-ce-que ça fait?"

"The poor girl is mad about Aylmer. He doesn't seem to know it, but he makes her worse by his indifference," Edith said.

"Why aren't you jealous of her, ma chère? No, I won't ask you that— the answer is obvious."

"I mean this, that if I can't ever do what he wishes, I feel she could make him happy; and I could bear it if she did."

"Spanish?" said Landi, as if to himself. "Olé! olé! Does she use the castanets, and wear a mantilla instead of a cap?"

"How frivolous and silly you are. No, of course not. She looks quite English, in fact particularly so."

"And yet you insist she's Spanish! Well, my advice is this. If he has a secret alliance with Spain, you should assume the Balkan attitude."

"Good gracious! What's that?"

"We're talking politics," said Landi, across the table. "Politics, and geography! Fancy, Meetchel, Mrs. Ottley doesn't know anything about the Balkans!"

"Ha, very good," said Mitchell. "Capital. What a fellow you are!" He gave his hearty, clubbable laugh. Mr. Mitchell belonged to an exceptionally large number of clubs and was a favourite at all. His laugh was the chief cause of his popularity there.

"Il est fou," said Landi quietly to Edith. "Quel monde! I don't think there are half-a-dozen sane people at this table."

"Oh, Landi!"

"And if there are, they shouldn't by rights be admitted into decent society. But the dear Meetchels don't know that; it's not public. I adore them both," he went on, changing his satirical tone, and again apparently drinking the health of Mrs. Mitchell, who waved her hand coquettishly from the end of the long table.

"Now listen, my child. Don't see Aylmer for a little while."

"He wants me to take him out for a drive."

"Take him for a drive. But not this week. How Madame Frabelle loves Bruce!" he went on, watching her.

"Really, Landi, I assure you you're occasionally as mistaken as she is. And she thinks I'm in love with our host."

"That's because *elle voit double*. I don't."

"What makes you think. . ."

"I read between the lines, my dear—between the lines on Madame Frabelle's face."

"She hasn't any."

"Oh, go along," said Landi, who sometimes broke into peculiar English which he thought was modern slang. Raising his voice, he said: "The dinner is *exquis—exquis*," so that Mr. Mitchell could hear.

"I can't help noting what you've eaten tonight, Landi, though I don't usually observe these things," Edith said. "You've had half-a-tomato, a small piece of vegetable marrow, and a sip of claret. Aren't you going to eat anything more?"

"Not much more. I look forward to my coffee and my cigar. Oh, how I look forward to it!"

"You know very well, Landi, they let you smoke cigarettes between the courses, if you like."

"It would be better than nothing. We'll see presently."

"Might I inquire if you live on cigars and coffee?"

"No," he answered satirically; "I live on eau sucré. And porreege. I'm Scotch."

"I can't talk to you if you're so silly."

"You'll tell me the important part on the little sofa upstairs in the salon," he said. "After dinner. Tonight, here, somehow, the food and the faces distract one—unless one is making an acquaintance. I know you too well to talk at dinner."

"Quite true. I ought to take time to think then."

"There's no hurry. Good heavens! the man has waited four years; he can wait another week. Quelle idée!"

"He's going back," said Edith, "as soon as he's well. He wants me to promise before he goes."

"Does he! You remind me of the man who said to his wife: 'Good-bye, my dear, I'm off to the Thirty Years' War.' It's all right, Edith. We'll find a solution, I have no fears."

She turned to Mr. Mitchell.

THE REST OF THE EVENING passed pleasantly. Alone with the women, Madame Frabelle was the centre of an admiring circle, as she lectured on "dress and economy in war-time," and how to manage a house on next to nothing a year. All the ladies gasped with admiration. Edith especially was impressed; because the fact that Madame Frabelle was a guest, and was managing nothing, did not prevent her talking as if she had any amount of experience on the subject, although, by her own showing she had been staying at hotels ever since the war began, except the last weeks she had spent with the Ottleys.

The men soon joined them.

A group of war valetudinarians, amongst whom Bruce was not the least emphatic, told each other their symptoms in a quiet corner. They described their strange shiverings down the spine; the curious fits of hunger that came on before meals; the dislike to crossing the road when there was an accident; the inability to sleep, sometimes taking the form of complete insomnia for as much as twenty minutes in the early morning. They pitied each other cordially, though neither listened to the other's symptoms, except in exchange for sympathy with their own.

"The war has got on my nerves; I can't think of anything else," Bruce said. "It's an *idée fixe*. I pant for the morning when the newspaper's due, and then I can't look at it! Not even a glance! Odd, isn't it?"

The Rev. Byrne Fraser, who gave his wife great and constant anxiety by his fantasies, related how he had curious dreams—the distressing part of which was that they never came true—about the death of relatives at the front. Another man also had morbid fancies on the subject of the casualty list, and had had to go and stay at a farm so as to "get right away from it all". But he soon left, as he had found, to his great disappointment, that his companions there were not intellectual, and could not even talk politics or discuss literature. And yet they went in (or so he had heard) for "intensive culture"! . . .

Presently Sir Tito played his Italian march. The musical portion of the party, and the unmusical alike, joined in the chorus. Then the party received a welcome addition. Valdez, the great composer, who had written many successful operas and had lived so much abroad that he cared now for nothing but British music, looked in after a patriotic concert given in order to help the unengaged professionals. Always loyal to old friends, he had deserted royalty itself tonight to greet Mrs. Mitchell and was persuaded by adoring ladies to sing his celebrated old song, "After Several Years." It pleased and thrilled the audience even more than Landi's "Adieu Hiver". Indeed, tonight it was Valdez who was the success of the evening. Middle-aged ladies who had loved him for years loved him now more than ever. Young girls who saw him now for the first time fell in love, just as their mothers had done, with his splendid black eyes and commanding presence, and secretly longed to stroke at least every seventh wave of his abundant hair. When Edith assured him that his curls were "like a flock of goats on Mount Gilead" he laughed, declared he was much flattered at the comparison, and kissed her hand with courtly grace.

Young Mr. Cricker, who came because he wasn't asked, insisted on dancing like Nijinsky because he was begged not to, but his leaps and bounds were soon stopped by a few subalterns and very young officers on leave, who insisted, with some fair partners, on dancing the Fox Trot to the sound of a gramophone.

For a few moments on the little sofa Edith managed to convey the rest of her confidence to Landi. She pointed out how hurried, how urgent, how pressing it was to give an answer.

"He wants a war elopement, I see," said Landi. "Mais ça ne se fait pas!"

"Then what am I to say?"

"Rien."

"But, Landi, you know I shan't really ever. . ."

"Would it give you pleasure to see him married to the Spanish girl?"

"She's not exactly Spanish—she only looks it. Don't laugh like that!"

"I don't know why, but Spain seems always to remind me of something ridiculous. Onions—or guitars."

"Well, I shouldn't mind her nearly so much as anyone else."

"You don't mind her," said Landi. "Vous savez qu'il ne l'épouse pas? What would you dislike him to do most?"

"I think I couldn't bear anyone else to take my place exactly," admitted Edith.

"C'est ça! you don't want him to be in love with another married woman with a husband like Bruce? Well, my dear, he won't. There is no other husband like Bruce."

Landi promised to consider the question, and she arranged to go and see him at his studio before seeing Aylmer again.

As they went out of the house Miss Coniston ran after Madame Frabelle and said eagerly:

"Oh, do tell me again; you say *soupe à la vinaigre* is marvellously nourishing and economical. I can have it made for my brother at our flat?"

"Of course you can! It costs next to nothing."

Arthur Coniston came up.

"And tastes like nothing on earth, I suppose?" he grumbled in his sister's ear. "You can't give me much less to eat than you do already."

"Oh, Arthur!" his sister said. "Aren't you happy at home? I think you're a pessimist."

"A pessimist!" cried Mitchell, who was following them into the hall. "Oh, I hate pessimists! What's the latest definition of them? Ah, I know; an optimist is a person who doesn't care what happens as long as it doesn't happen to him."

"Yes," said Edith quickly, "and a pessimist is the person who lives with the optimist."

"Dear, dear. I always thought the old joke was that an optimist looks after the eyes, and a pessimist after the feet!" cried Madame Frabelle as she fastened her cloak.

"Why, then, he ought to go to a cheer-upadist!" said Mr. Mitchell. And they left him in roars of laughter.

XVIII

D ulcie Clay, in her neat uniform of grey and white, with the scarlet cross on the front of her apron, was sitting in the room she occupied for the moment in Aylmer's house in Jermyn Street. It was known as "the second best bedroom". As she was anxious not to behave as if she were a guest, she used it as a kind of boudoir when she was not in attendance.

It was charmingly furnished in the prim Chippendale style, a style dainty, but not luxurious, that seemed peculiarly suited to Dulcie.

She was in the window-seat—not with her feet up, no cushions behind her. Unlike Edith, she was not the kind of woman who rested habitually; she sat quite upright in the corner. A beautiful little mahogany table was at her right, with a small electric lamp on it, and two books. One of the books was her own choice, the other had been lent to her by Aylmer. It was a volume of Bernard Shaw. She could make neither head nor tail of it, and the prefaces, which she read with the greatest avidity, perplexed her even more than the books themselves. Every now and then a flash of lightning, in the form of some phrase she knew, illumined for a second the darkness of the author's words. But soon she closed the thick volume with the small print and returned to *The Daisy Chain*.

Dulcie was barely one-and-twenty. She carried everywhere in her trunk a volume called *The Wide, Wide World*. She was never weary of reading this work with the comprehensive title; it reminded her of schooldays. It was comforting, like a dressing-gown and slippers, like an old friend. Whether she had ever thoroughly understood it may be doubted. If any modern person nowadays were to dip into it, he would find it, perhaps, more obscure than George Meredith at his darkest. Secretly Dulcie loved best in the world, in the form of reading matter, the feuilletons in the daily papers. There was something so exciting in that way they have of stopping at a thrilling moment and leaving you the whole day to think over what would come next, and the night to sleep over it. She preferred that; she never concentrated her mind for long on a story, or any work of the imagination. She was deeply interested in her own life. She was more subjective than objective—though, perhaps, she had never heard the words. Unconsciously she dealt with life only as it related to herself. But this is almost universal with young girls who have only just become conscious of themselves, and of their importance in the world; have only just left the simple objectiveness of the child who wants to look at the world, and have barely begun to feel what it is to be an actor rather than a spectator.

Not that any living being could be less selfish or vain, or less of an egotist than Dulcie. If she saw things chiefly as they were related to herself, it was because this problem of her life was rather an intricate one. Her position was not sufficiently simple to suit her simple nature.

Her mother, who had been of Spanish descent, had died young; her father had married again. He was the sort of man who always married again, and if his present wife, with whom he was rather in love, had passed away he would have undoubtedly married a third time. Some men are born husbands; they have a passion for domesticity, for a fireside, for a home. Yet, curiously, these men very rarely stay at home. Apparently what they want is to have a place to get away from.

The new stepmother, who was young and rather pretty, was not unkind, but was bored and indifferent to the little girl. Dulcie was sensitive; since her father's second marriage she had always felt in the way. Whether her stepmother was being charming to her husband, or to some other man—she was always charming to somebody—Dulcie felt continually that she was not wanted. Her father was kind and casual. He told everyone what he believed, that his second wife was an ideal person to bring up his little daughter.

Therefore it came upon him as a surprise when she told him she was grown up, and still more that she wished to leave home and be a nurse. Mrs. Clay had made no objection; the girl rather depressed her, for she felt she ought to like her more than she did, so she "backed up" with apparent good nature the great desire to go out and do something.

Dulcie had inherited three hundred a year from her mother. Her father had about the same amount of his own to live on. He believed that he added to it by mild gambling, and perhaps by talking a good deal at his club of how he had been born to make a fortune but had had no luck. His second wife had no money.

Dulcie, therefore, was entirely independent. No obstacles were placed in her way—the particular form that her ambition took was suggested by the war, but in any case she would have done something. She had taken the usual means of getting into a hospital.

Gentle, industrious, obedient and unselfish, she got on well. Her prettiness gained her no enemies among the women as she was too serious about her work at this time to make use of her beauty by attracting men. Yet Dulcie was unusually feminine; she had a natural gift for nursing, for housekeeping, for domesticity. She was not artistic and was as indifferent to abstractions and to general ideas as the ideal average woman. She was tactful, sweet, and, she had been called at school, rather a doormat. Her appearance was distinguished and she was not at all ordinary. It is far from ordinary, indeed it is very rare, to be the ideal average woman. She took great interest in detail; she would lie awake at night thinking about how she would go the next day to a certain inexpensive shop to get a piece of ribbon for one part of her dress to match a piece of ribbon in another part—neither of which would ever be seen by any human being.

Such men as she saw liked and admired her. Her gradual success led her to being sent abroad to a military hospital. She inspired confidence, not because she had initiative, but because one knew she would do exactly as she was told, which is, in itself, a great quality. At Boulogne she made the acquaintance at once of Aylmer, and of *the coup de foudre*. She worshipped him at first sight. So she thought herself fortunate when she was allowed to come back to London with him. Under orders she continued her assiduous attention. Everyone said she was a perfect nurse.

Occasionally she went to see her father. He greeted her with warmth and affection, and told her all about how, on account of racing being stopped, he was gradually becoming a pauper. When she began telling him of the events in which she was absorbed he answered by giving her news of the prospects for the Cambridgeshire. In the little den in the house in West Kensington, where he lived, she would come in and say in a soft voice:

"Papa dear, you know I shan't be able to stop much longer."

"Much longer where?"

"Why, with my patient, Mr. Ross—Mr. Aylmer Ross."

"Shan't you? Mind you, my dear, there are two good three-year-olds that are not to be sneezed at." He shook his head solemnly.

It had never occurred to Dulcie for a moment to sneeze at three-year-olds. She hardly knew what they were.

"But what do you advise for me, papa?"

"My dear child, I can't advise. You can't select with any approach to confidence between Buttercup and Beautiful Doll. Mind you, I'm very much inclined to think that More Haste may win yet. Look how he ran in August, when nobody knew anything about him!"

"Yes, I know, papa, but—"

She gave it up.

"Go and see your mother, dear; go and ask her about it," and he returned to the racing intelligence.

Strange that a man who had not enough to live on should think he could add to his income by backing losers. Still, such was Mr. Clay's view of life. Besides, he was just going out; he was always just going out.

She would then go and see her stepmother, who greeted her most affectionately.

Dulcie only kept half her little income for herself at present, a considerable advantage to a woman like Mrs. Clay, who declared she was "expected to dress up to a certain standard, though, of course, simply during war-time." She would kiss the girl and drag her up to her bedroom to show her a new coat and skirt, or send the general servant up to bring down the marvellously cheap little tea-gown that had just come home.

Both her parents, it will be seen, were ready enough to talk to her, but they were not prepared to listen. All the warmth and affection that she had in her nature very naturally was concentrated on her patient.

Dulcie now sat in the window-seat, wondering what to do. She was sadly thinking what would happen when the time came for her to leave.

In her mind she knew perfectly well that what several people had said was true: the profession she had chosen was too arduous for her physical strength. Besides, now she could not bear the idea of nursing anyone else after Aylmer. She was trying to make up her mind to take something else—and she could not think what.

A girl like Dulcie Clay, who has studied only one thing really thoroughly, could be fitted only to be a companion either to children, whom she adored, or to some tedious elderly lady with fads. She knew she would not do for a secretary; she had not the education nor the gift for it.

The thought of going back to the stepmother who showed so clearly her satisfaction and high spirits in having got rid of her, and of being again the unwanted third in the little house in West Kensington, was quite unbearable.

She had told much of her position to Edith, who was so sympathetic and clever. It would have been a dream of hers, a secret dream, to teach Edith's little girl, whom she had once seen, and loved. Yet that would have been in some ways rather difficult. As she looked out of the window, darkened with fog, she sighed. If she had been the governess at Edith's house, she would be constantly seeing Aylmer. She knew, of course, all about Aylmer's passion. It would certainly be better than nothing to see him sometimes. But the position would have been painful. Also, she disliked Bruce. He had given her one or two looks that seemed rather to demand admiration than to express it; he had been so kind as to give her a few hints on nursing; how to look after a convalescent; and had been exceedingly frank and kind in confiding to her his own symptoms. As she was a hospital nurse, it seemed to him natural to talk rather of his own indisposition than on any other subject. Dulcie was rather highly strung, and Bruce got terribly on her nerves; she marvelled at Edith's patience. But then Edith. . . No, she could not go to the Ottleys.

Her other gift—a beautiful soprano voice—also was of hardly any use to her, as she was now placed. When she sang she expressed herself more completely than at any other time, but that also she had not been taught thoroughly; she had been taught nothing thoroughly.

A companion! Though she had not absolutely to earn her living, and kept only half of her little inheritance for herself, what was to become of her? Well, she wouldn't think about it any more that day. At any rate Aylmer talked as though she was to remain some time longer.

When he had returned suddenly to the house in Jermyn Street, a relative had hastily obtained for him the necessary servants; his former valet was at the front; they were all new to him and to his ways, and he had no housekeeper. Dulcie did the housekeeping—could she take that place in his house? No, she knew that she was too young, and everyone else would have said she was too pretty. Only as a nurse would it be correct for her to be his companion.

And from fear of embarrassing him she was hardly ever with him alone. She thought he was abrupt, more cool to her since their return, and guessed the reason; it was for fear of compromising her. How angelic of him; what a wonderful man—how fortunate his first wife must have been. And the boy, Teddy—the charming boy so like his father, whom she had only seen for a day or two before he left to go out. Teddy's presence would help to make it more difficult for her to remain.

In that very short time the boy had distinctly shown her by his marked attention how much he admired her. He thought her lovely. He was devoted to music and she had sung to him.

Aylmer also liked music, but apparently did not care to hear her sing. On the occasion that she did, it seemed to irritate him. Indeed, she knew she was merely the most amateurish of musicians, and could just accompany herself in a few songs, though the voice itself was a rare gift. . . How perfect Aylmer had been! . . . There was a sharp ring. She closed the book, turned out the little electric lamp and went downstairs.

She was looking ideally pretty in the becoming uniform, but uniforms are always becoming, whatever the uniforms or the people may be. The reason of this is too obscure to fathom. One would say that to dress to suit oneself would be more becoming to men and women. Yet, in fact, the limitation and the want of variety in this sort of dress had a singular attraction. However, if she had chosen it to suit her, nothing could have been more becoming. The severity of the form, the dull colour, relieved by the large scarlet cross, showed off to the greatest advantage her dense dark hair, her Madonna-like face and the slim yet not angular lines of her figure. Dulcie's beauty was of a kind that is thrown into relief by excessive plainness of dress.

XIX

As she came in, Aylmer looked at her with more observation than usual, and he acknowledged to himself that she was pretty—remarkably pretty, quite a picture, as people say, and he liked her, as one likes a confidante, a reliable friend. He trusted her, remembering how he had given himself away to her that dreadful day in the Boulogne hospital. . . And she had another quality that pleased him immensely; she was neither coquettish nor affected, but simple and serious. She appeared to think solely of her duties, and in Aylmer's opinion that was just what a nurse should do.

BUT EDITH'S REMARK THAT DULCIE was madly in love with him had made a certain impression on his mind. Indeed, everything Edith said, even a merely trivial observation, was of importance to Aylmer. Edith wouldn't have said that unless she meant it. If it was true, did it matter? Aylmer was very free from vanity and masculine coquetry. He had a good deal of pride and great self-respect. Like almost every human being who is superior to the average, he didn't think ill of himself; there were things that he was proud of. He was proud, secretly, of having gone into the army and of having been wounded. It made him feel he was not on the shelf, not useless and superannuated. He took a certain pride also in his judgement, his excellent judgement on pictures and literature. Perhaps, even, having been a spoilt only child, he was privately proud of some of his faults. He knew he was extravagant and impatient. The best of everything was barely good enough for Aylmer. Long before he inherited the property that had come to him a year ago he had never been the sort of young man who would manage on little; who would, for example, go to the gallery by Underground or omnibus to see a play or to the opera. He required comfort, elbow-room, ease. For that reason he had worked really hard at the Bar so as to have enough money to live according to his ideas. Not that he took any special interest in the Bar. His ideal had always been—if it could be combined—to be either a soldier or a man of leisure, devoted to sport, literature and art.

Now he had asserted himself as a soldier, and he meant to go back. But he looked forward to leisure to enjoy and indulge his favourite tastes, if possible, with the only woman he had ever been deeply in love with.

ADA LEVERSON

He was particularly attractive to women, who liked his strong will and depth of feeling, his assertive manner and that feeling of trust that he inspired. Women always know when a man will not treat them badly. Teddy's mother, his first wife, he had really married out of pity.

When she died everyone regarded it as a tragedy except himself. He still worshipped his mother, whose little miniature he kept always by him, and he had always fancied that Edith resembled her. This was simply an *idée d'amoureux*, for there was no resemblance. His mother, according to the miniature, had the dark hair and innocent expression that were the fashion at the time, while Edith was fair, with rather dark eyebrows, grey eyes and the mouth and chin characteristic of Burne-Jones's and Rossetti's pictures. But though she might be in appearance a Burne-Jones, she was very modern. His favourite little photograph of her that he had shown, in his moment of despair, to Dulcie, showed a charming face, sensuous yet thoughtful, under a large hat. She had fur up to her chin, and was holding a muff; it was a snapshot taken the winter before they had parted.

Aylmer worshipped these two women: his dead mother and the living woman whom he had never given up entirely. How unlike were both the types to Dulcie Clay, with her waved Madonna hair, dark skin, large, clear blue eyes, softened by eyelashes of extraordinary length. Her chin was very small, her mouth fine, rather thin; she had a pathetic expression; one could imagine her attending, helping, nursing, holding a child in her arms, but not his intellectual equal, guiding and directing like his mother; and without the social brilliance and charm of Edith.

SEEING HIM LOOKING AT HER with a long, observant look, Dulcie became nervous and trembled slightly. She waited for him to speak.

"Come here, Miss Clay. I want to speak to you."

Instantly she sat down by him.

"I wanted to say—you've been most awfully kind to me."

Dulcie murmured something.

"I'm nearly well now—aren't I?"

"Dr. Wood says you can go out driving next week."

"Yes; but I don't mean that. I mean, I'm well in myself?"

He spoke quickly, almost impatiently.

"The doctor says you're still suffering from nervous shock;" she answered in a toneless voice, professionally.

"Still, very soon I shan't need any attendance that a valet or a housekeeper couldn't give me, shall I?"

"No, I suppose not."

"Well, my dear Miss Clay—of course, I shall hate you to go," he said politely, "but don't you think we ought to be thinking—"

He stopped.

She answered:

"Of course I'll go whenever you and Dr. Wood think it right."

"You see," he went on, "I know I shall need a housekeeper, especially when Teddy comes back. He's coming back on leave next week"— Aylmer glanced at the telegram in his hand—"and, well—"

"You don't think I could—"

"Of course you would make a splendid housekeeper," he laughed. "You are already, but—"

She didn't wish to make him uncomfortable. Evidently he was thinking what she knew herself. But she was so reluctant to go.

"Don't you think I could remain here for a little while?" she said modestly. "To do the housekeeping and be useful? You see, I've nowhere to go really."

"But, my dear girl, excuse me, don't you see you're rather too—young. It would be selfish of me to let you."

He wished to say that it would be compromising, but a certain consciousness prevented his saying it. He felt he would be ridiculous if he put it into words.

"Just as you like. How soon do you think I ought to go?"

Though she tried not to show it, there was a look almost of despair in her face. Her eyes looked startled, as if trying not to shed tears.

He was very sorry for her, but tried to hide it by a cool and impatient manner.

"Well, shall we say in about a fortnight?"

"Certainly." She looked down.

"I shall miss you awfully," he said, speaking more quickly than usual to get it over.

She gave a very small smile.

"Er—and then may I ask what you're thinking of doing next?"

"That was just what I was thinking about," she answered rather naïvely. "There are so few things I can do."

Then fearing this sentence sounded like begging to remain, she hastily added:

"And of course if I don't go home I might be a companion or look after children."

"I wonder if Mrs. Ottley—" began Aylmer. "She has a dear little girl, and I've heard her say she would soon want someone."

"Dilly?" said Dulcie, with a slight smile.

"Yes, Dilly."

There was a moment of intense awkwardness between them.

Then Dulcie said:

"I'm afraid that wouldn't quite do. I'm not clever enough."

"Oh, rot. You know enough for a child like that. I shall speak to Mrs. Ottley about it."

"It's very, very kind of you, but I would rather not. I think I shall try to be a companion."

"What's the name of that woman," Aylmer said good-naturedly, "that Irish woman, wife of one of the Cabinet Ministers, who came to the hospital at Boulogne and wanted to have lessons?"

"Lady Conroy," Dulcie answered.

"Yes, Lady Conroy. Supposing that she needed a secretary or companion, would you dislike that?"

"Oh, no, I should like it very much."

"Right. I'll get Mrs. Ottley to speak to her about it. She said she was coming to London, didn't she?"

"Yes. I got to know her fairly well," said Dulcie. "She's very charming."

"She's celebrated for her bad memory," Aylmer said, with a smile.

"She declares she forgets her own name sometimes. Once she got into a taxi and told the man to drive home. When he asked where that was, she said it was his business to know. She had forgotten her address."

They both laughed.

"I'll go tomorrow," said Dulcie, "and see my stepmother, if you don't want me in the afternoon. Or, perhaps, the day you go for a drive would be better."

"Tell me, Miss Clay, aren't you happy at home?"

"Oh, it isn't that. They don't want me. I'm in the way. You see, they've got used to my being out of the house."

"But, excuse me—you don't earn your own living really?"

"No, that isn't really necessary. But I don't want to live at home."

Her face showed such a decided distaste to the idea that he said no more.

"You're looking very well today," Dulcie said.

He sighed. "I feel rather rotten. I can't read, can't settle to anything."

She looked at him sympathetically. He felt impelled to go on.

"I'm a bit worried," he continued.

"About your son?"

"No, not about him so much, though I wish he would get a flesh wound and be sent back," his father said, laughing. "But about myself."

She looked at him in silence.

"You know—what I told you."

She made no answer, looking away to give him time to speak.

"I've made a suggestion," he said slowly. . . "If it's accepted it'll alter all my life. Of course I shall go out again. But still it will alter my life."

Suddenly, overpowered by the longing for sympathy, he said to himself aloud.

"I wonder if there's a chance."

"I don't know what it is," she murmured, but instinctively she had guessed something of it.

"I don't want to think about it any more at present."

"Shall I read to you?"

"Yes, do."

She quietly arranged a pillow behind him and took up a newspaper.

He often liked her to read to him; he never listened to a word of it, but it was soothing.

She had taken up "This Morning's Gossip" from *The Daily Mail*, and she began in the soft, low, distinct voice reading from The Rambler:

"Lord Redesdale says that when Lord Haldane's scheme for a Territorial Army was on foot he took it to the—"

Aylmer stopped her.

"No—not that"

"Shall I read you a novel?"

"I think I should like to hear some poetry today," he answered.

She had taken up a pretty, tiny little book that lay on his table, called *Lyrists of the Restoration*, and began to read aloud:

> *"Phyllis is my only joy,*
> *Faithless as the winds or seas,*
> *Sometimes cunning, sometimes coy,*
> *Yet she never fails to please."*

"Oh, please, stop," Aylmer cried.

She looked up.

"It tinkles like an old-fashioned musical-box. Try another."

"What would you like?" she asked, smiling.

He took up a French book and passed it to her.

"You'll think I'm very changeable, but I should like this. Read me the beginning of *La-Bos*."

And she began.

He listened with his eyes closed, lulled by the curious technique, with its constant repetitions and jewelled style, charmed altogether. She read French fluently enough.

"That's delightful," he said, but he soon noticed she was stumbling over the words. No, it was not suitable for her to read. He was obstinate, however, and was determined she should read him something.

So they fell back on *Northanger Abbey*.

XX

Lady Conroy had arrived home in Carlton House Terrace, complaining of a headache. She remained on the sofa in her sitting-room for about five minutes, during which time she believed she had been dozing. In reality she had been looking for her glasses, dropping her bag and ringing the bell to send a servant for a handkerchief.

She was a handsome woman of thirty-eight, with black hair turning a little grey, grey Irish eyes and a wonderfully brilliant complexion. She must have been a remarkably good-looking girl, but now, to her great vexation, she was growing a little too fat. She varied between treatments, which she scarcely began before she forgot them, and utter indifference to her appearance, when she declared she was much happier, letting herself go in loose gowns, and eating everything of which she had deprived herself for a day or two for the sake of her figure.

Lady Conroy had often compared herself to the old woman who lived in a shoe, because of her large family. Her friends declared she didn't remember how many children she had. She loved them, but there were certainly weeks when she didn't see the younger ones, for she was constantly absorbed in various different subjects. Besides, she spent most of her life in looking for things.

She was hopelessly careless and had no memory at all.

Suddenly she glanced at the watch on her wrist, compared it with the splendid Empire clock on the mantelpiece, and went with a bewildered look to the telephone on her writing-desk. Having gone through a considerable amount of torture by calling up the wrong number and absently ringing off as soon as she had got the right one, she at last found herself talking to Edith.

"Oh, is that you, dear? How lucky to catch you! Yes. . . Yes. . . I came back yesterday. Dying to see you. Can't you come round and see me? Oh, you've got on your hat; you were just coming? Of course, I forgot! I knew I had an appointment with someone! How soon will you be here? . . . In a quarter of an hour? Good! Could you tell me the time, dear? . . . Four o'clock, thanks. My watch is wrong, and they've never wound the clock up all the time I've been away. Good-bye. Don't be long. . . How soon did you say you could come? . . . Oh, about a quarter of an hour! Do hurry! . . . I say, I've something very particular to tell you. It's about. . . Oh, I'm detaining you. Very well. I see. Au revoir."

As she waited for her visitor, Lady Conroy walked round the room. Nearly everything on which she cast her eye reminded her of a different train of thought, so that by the time Edith was announced by the footman she had forgotten what she wanted to tell her.

"How sweet you look, dear!" cried Lady Conroy, welcoming her most affectionately. "How dear of you to come. You can't think how I was longing to see you. Can you tell me what day it is?"

"Why, it's Thursday," Edith said, laughing. "Don't you remember? You wired to me to come and see you today."

"Of course; so I did. But, surely, I didn't ask you to come on Thursday?"

"I assure you that you did."

"Fancy! How stupid of me! Thursday is my day at home. Dear, dear, dear. I forgot to tell Standing; there will be no proper tea. Oh, I've brought such a nice French maid—a perfect wonder. She knows everything. She always knows what I want. One moment, dear; I'll ring for her and give her orders. Wait a minute, though." She took Edith's hand and patted it affectionately. "Nobody knows I've come back; it'll be all right. We shan't have any visitors. I'm bursting with news to tell you."

"And I'm longing to hear what it is."

Lady Conroy's charming, animated face became blank. She frowned slightly, and a vague look came into her eyes—the pathetic look of someone who is trying to remember.

"Wait a minute—what is it? Oh yes. You know that woman you introduced me to at Dieppe?"

"What woman?"

"Don't you know, dear? Good heavens, it was you who introduced her—you ought to know."

"Do you mean Madame Frabelle?" asked Edith, who was accustomed to Lady Conroy, and could follow the drift of her mind.

"Capital! That's it. How wonderful of you! Yes, Madame Frabelle. How do you like her?"

"Very much. But I didn't introduce her to you. You sent her to me."

"Did I? Well, it's very much the same. Look here, Edith dear. This is what I want to ask you. I remember now. Oh, do you mind ringing the bell for me? I must tell Marie about the tea, in case people call."

Edith obeyed.

"You see, dear," went on her hostess, "I've undertaken a terrific number of things—Belgian refugees, weekly knitting, hundreds of societies—all sorts of war work. Well, you know how busy I am, even without all that, don't you? Thank heaven the boys are at school, but there are the children in the nursery, and I don't leave them—at least hardly ever—to their nurse. I look after them myself—when I think of it. Oh, they've grown such heavenly angels—too sweet! And how's your pet, Dilly?"

"Very well. But do go on."

"How right of you to keep me to the point, darling. That's where you're such a comfort always. Do you mind passing me my glasses? Thanks."

She put them on and immediately took them off. She only needed them for reading.

"Oh yes. I wanted to consult you about something, Edith."

The footman came in.

"Oh, Standing, send Marie to me at once. . . Bother the man, how he keeps worrying! Well, Edith dear, as I've got all this tremendous lot of work to do, I've made up my mind, for the sake of my health, I simply must have a sort of secretary or companion. You see?"

"I quite see. You spoke of it before."

"Well, how do you think that woman you introduced to me, Madame Frabelle—how do you think she would—? Oh, Marie, today's my day at home; isn't it, Edith?"

"Today is Thursday," said Edith.

"Thursday! Oh, my dear. Thursday's not my day at home. Well, anyhow, never mind about that. What was I saying, Marie?"

Marie remained respectfully waiting, with a tight French smile on her intelligent face.

"Oh, I know what it was. Marie, I want you to look after certain things for me here—anyhow, at present. I want you to tell the cook that I want tea at four o'clock. Oh no, it's half-past four—well, at five. And there's something I particularly want for tea. What is it?" she asked, looking at Edith. Immediately answering herself she said: "I know, I want muffins."

"Madame want 'nuffing'?" said Marie.

"No, no, no! Don't be so stupid. It's an English thing, Marie; you wouldn't understand. Something I've forgotten to tell the cook about. It's so cosy I always think in the winter in London. It always cheers me up. You know, what is it? . . . I know—muffins—*muffins!*" she said the word carefully to the French maid.

Edith came to the rescue.

"Tell the cook," she said, "for madame, that she wants some muffins for tea."

"Oh, oui. Ah, oui, bien, madame. Merci, madame."

As the maid was going away Lady Conroy called out:

"Oh, tell the cook it doesn't matter. I won't have them today."

"Bien, madame."

Edith was already in a somewhat hilarious mood. Lady Conroy didn't irritate her; she amused her almost more than any friend she had. Besides, once she could be got to concentrate on any one subject, nobody was more entertaining. Edith's English humour delighted in her friend's Irish wit.

There was something singularly Irish in the way Lady Conroy managed to make a kind of muddle and untidiness all round her, when she had been in a room a minute or two. When she had entered the room, it was a fine-looking apartment, rather sparsely furnished, with very little in it, all severest First Empire style. There were a few old portraits on striped pale green walls, and one large basket of hot-house flowers on a small table. Yet, since her entrance, the room already looked as if several people had been spending the week in it without tidying it up. Almost mechanically Edith picked up her bag, books, newspaper, cigarettes and the glasses.

"Well, then, you don't think Madame Frabelle would do?" said Lady Conroy.

"My dear Lady Conroy, Madame Frabelle wouldn't dream of going as a companion or secretary. You want a young girl. She's about fifteen years older than you are and she's staying with me as my guest. I shouldn't even suggest such a thing."

"Why not? It wouldn't be at all a hard place."

"No, I know. But she doesn't want a place. She's very well off, remember."

"Good heavens, she can't have much to do then if she's only staying with you," said Lady Conroy.

"Oh, she has plenty of engagements. No, I shouldn't advise Madame Frabelle. But I do know of someone."

"Do you? Oh, darling Edith, how sweet of you. Oh, just ring the bell for me, will you?"

Edith rang.

"I want to send for Marie, my maid, and tell her to order some muffins for tea. I forgot to tell the cook."

"But you have already ordered and countermanded them."

"Oh, have I?—so I have! Never mind, don't ring. It doesn't matter. Who do you know, dear?"

Standing appeared in answer to the bell.

"What do you want, Standing? You mustn't keep bothering and interrupting me like this. Oh, tea? Yes, bring tea. And tell Marie I shan't want her after all."

Lady Conroy leant back against her cushions and with a sigh went on:

"You see, I'm in the most terrible muddle, dear Edith. I don't know where to turn."

She turned to her writing-table and opened it.

"Look at this, now," she said rather triumphantly. "This is all about my war work. Oh no, it isn't. It's an advertisement from a washer-woman. Gracious, ought I to keep it, do you think? No, I don't think I need."

She folded it up and put it carefully away again.

"Don't you think yourself I need someone?"

"Yes, I do. I think it would be very convenient for you to have a nice girl with a good memory to keep your things in order."

"That's it," cried Lady Conroy, delighted, as she lit a cigarette. "That's it—someone who will prevent me dropping cigarette ash all over the room and remember my engagements and help me with my war work and write my letters and do the telephoning. That's all I shall want. Of course, if she could do a little needlework—No, no, that wouldn't do. You couldn't expect her to do brainwork as well as needlework."

Edith broke in.

"Do you remember mentioning to me a girl you met at Boulogne—a nurse called Dulcie Clay?"

"Perfectly well," answered Lady Conroy, puffing away at her cigarette, and obviously not speaking the truth.

Edith laughed.

"No, my dear, you don't. But it doesn't matter. Well, this girl has been nursing Mr. Aylmer Ross, and he doesn't need her any more—at least he won't after next week. Would you see her and judge for yourself? You might try her."

"I'm sure I shall if I take her. I'm afraid I'm a trying person. I try everyone dreadfully. Oh, by the way, Edith, I met such a perfect angel coming over. He was a wounded soldier. He belongs to the Black Watch.

Doesn't the name Black Watch thrill you? He's in the Irish Guards, so, of course, my heart went out to him."

"The Irish Guards as well?"

"Oh no. That was another man."

She put her hand to her forehead.

"I'm worrying you, dear, with my bad memory. I'm so sorry. Well, then, you'll see Madame Frabelle for me?"

"I will if you like, but not as a companion. It's Miss Clay."

"Miss Clay," repeated Lady Conroy. "Ah, here's tea. Do you take milk and sugar. Edith?"

"Let me pour it out," said Edith, to whom it was maddening to see the curious things Lady Conroy did with the tea-tray. She was pouring tea into the sugar basin, looking up at Edith with the sweetest smile.

"I can't stay long," Edith went on. "I'm very sorry, dear, but you remember I told you I'm in a hurry. . . I've an appointment at Landi's studio."

"Landi? And who is that?"

"You know him—the composer—Sir Tito."

"Oh, darling Sir Tito! Of course I do know him!" She smiled reminiscently. "Won't you have anything to eat, dear? Do have a muffin! Oh, bother, there are none. I wonder how it is cook always forgets? Then you're going to send Madame Frabelle to see me the day after tomorrow?"

Edith took both her hands and shook them, laughing, as she stood up.

"I will arrange to send Miss Clay to see you, and if you like her, if you don't mind waiting about ten days or a fortnight, you might engage her. It would be doing her a great kindness. She's not happy at home."

"Oh, poor girl!"

"And she went as a nurse," continued Edith, "chiefly because she couldn't think of anything else to do. She isn't really strong enough for nursing."

"Isn't she? How sad, poor girl. It reminds me of a girl I met at Boulogne. So pretty and nice. In very much the same position really. She also wasn't happy at home—"

"This is the same girl," said Edith. "You wrote to me about her."

"Did I? Good heavens, how extraordinary! What a memory you've got, Edith. Well, then, she's sure to do."

"Still, you'd better have an interview," said Edith. "Don't trouble to ring. I must fly, dear. We'll soon meet again."

Lady Conroy followed her to the door into the hall, pouring forth questions, sympathy and cheerful communications about the charming young man in the Black Watch. Just before Edith escaped her friend said:

"Oh, by the by, I meant to ask you something. Who is Madame Frabelle?"

XXI

S ir Tito lived in a flat in Mayfair, on the second floor of a large corner house. On the ground floor was his studio, which had two entrances. The studio was a large, square, white room, containing a little platform for pupils. A narrow shelf ran all the way round the dado; this shelf was entirely filled with the most charming collection of English and French china, little cottages, birds and figures. Above the shelf was a picture-rail, which again was filled all the way round with signed photographs of friends. Everything in the room was white, even the piano was *laqué* white, and the furniture, extremely luxurious and comfortable, was in colour a pale and yet dull pink. A curtain separated it from another smaller room, which again had a separate entrance into the hall on the left, and, through a very small dressing-room, led into the street on the right side.

Sir Tito was waiting for Edith, spick, span and debonair as always (although during the war he had discarded his buttonhole). He was occupied, as he usually was in his leisure time, not in playing the piano or composing, but—in making photograph frames! This was his hobby, and people often said that he took more pleasure in the carving, cutting out, gumming and sticking together of these objects than in composing the melodies that were known and loved all over the world.

As soon as Edith came in he showed her a tiny frame carved with rosebuds.

"Regarde," he said, his eyes beaming. "Voilà! C'est mignon, n'est-ce-pas? On dirait un petit coeur! Ravissante, hein?" He gazed at it lovingly.

"Very sweet," said Edith, laughing. "Who is it for?"

"Why, it's for your *mignonne*, Dilly. I've cut out a photograph of hers in the shape of a heart. Gentil, n'est ce pas?"

He showed it to her with childish pleasure. Then he put all traces of the work carefully away in a drawer and drew Edith near to the fire.

"I've just a quarter of an hour to give you," said Sir Tito, suddenly turning into a serious man of business. And, indeed, he always had many appointments, not a few of which were on some subject connected with love affairs. Like Aylmer, but in a different way, Sir Tito was always being consulted, but, oddly enough, while it was the parents and guardians usually who went to Aylmer, husbands worried about their wives, mothers about their children; to the older man it was more frequently the culprit or the confidant himself or herself who came to confide and ask for help and advice.

Edith said:

"The dreadful thing I've to tell you, Landi, is that I've completely changed."

"Comment?"

"Yes. I'm in love with him all over again."

"C'est vrai?"

"Yes. I don't know how and I don't know why. When he first made that suggestion, it seemed wild—impossible. But the things he said—how absolutely true it is. Landi, my life's been wasted, utterly wasted."

Landi said nothing.

"I believe I was deceiving myself," she went on. "I've got so accustomed to living this sort of half life I've become almost *abrutie*, as you would say. I didn't realise how much I cared for him. Now I know I always adored him."

"But you were quite contented."

"Because I made myself so; because I resolved to be satisfied. But, after all, there's something in what he says, Landi. My life with Bruce is only a makeshift. Nothing but tact, tact, tact. Oh, I'm so tired of tact!" She sighed. "It seems to me now really too hard that I should again have such a great opportunity and should throw it away. You see, it is an opportunity, if I love him—and I'm not deceiving myself now. I'm in love with him. The more I think about it the more lovely it seems to me. It would be an ideal life, Landi."

He was still silent.

She continued:

"You see, Aylmer knows so well how much the children are to me, and he would never ask me to leave them. There's no question of my ever leaving them. And Bruce wouldn't mind. Bruce would be only too thankful for me to take them. And there's another thing—though I despised the idea at the time, there's a good deal in it. I mean that Aylmer's well off, so I should never be a burden. He would love to take the responsibility of us all. I would leave my income to Bruce; he would be quite comfortable and independent. Oh, he would take it. He might be a little cross, but it wouldn't last, Landi. He would be better off. He'd find somebody—someone who would look after him, perhaps, and make him quite happy and comfortable. You're shocked?"

"Ça ne m'étonne pas. It's the reaction," said Landi, nodding.

"How wonderful of you to understand! I haven't seen him again, you know. I've just been thinking. In fact, I'm surprised at myself. But the more I reflect on what he said, the more wonderful it seems. . . Think how he's cared for me all this time!"

"Sans doute. You know that he adores you. But, Edith, it's all very well—you put like that—but could you go through with it?"

"I believe I could now," she answered. "I begin to long to. You see, I mistook my own feelings, Landi; they seemed dulled. I thought I could live without love—but why should I? What is it that's made me change so? Why do I feel so frightened now at the idea of losing my happiness?"

"C'est la guerre," said Sir Tito.

"The war? What has that to do with it?"

"Everything. Unconsciously it affects people. Though you yourself are not fighting, Aylmer has risked his life, and is going to risk it again. This impresses you. To many temperaments things seem to matter less just now. People are reckless."

"Is it that?" asked Edith. "Perhaps it is. But I was so completely deceived in myself."

"I always knew you could be in love with him," said Landi. "But wait a moment, Edith—need the remedy be so violent? I don't ask you to live without love. Why should a woman live without the very thing she was created for? But you know you hate publicity—vulgar scandal. Nobody loathes it as you do."

"It doesn't seem to matter now so much," Edith said.

"It's the war."

"Well, whatever's the cause, all I can tell you is that I'm beginning to think I shall do it! I want to! . . . I can't bear to refuse again. I haven't seen him since our talk. I changed gradually, alone, just thinking. And then you say—"

"Many people have love in their lives without a violent public scandal," he repeated.

"Yes, I know. I understand what you mean. But I hate deceit, Landi. I don't think I could lead a double life. And even if I would, he wouldn't!"

She spoke rather proudly.

"Pauvre garçon!" said Sir Tito. "Je l'admire."

"So do I," said Edith. "Aylmer's not a man who could shake hands with Bruce and be friends and deceive him. And you know, before, when I begged him to remain. . . my friend. . . he simply wouldn't. He always said he despised the man who would accept the part of a tame cat. And he doesn't believe in Platonic friendship: Aylmer's too honest, too *real* for that."

"But, Edith, oh, remember, before," said Landi taking her hand, "even when Bruce ran away with another woman, you couldn't bear the idea of divorce."

"I know. But I may have been wrong. Besides, I didn't care for him as I do now. And I'm older now."

"Isn't this rather sudden, my dear?"

"Only because I've let myself go—let myself be natural! Oh, *do* encourage me—give me strength, Landi! Don't let me be a coward! Think if Aylmer goes out again and is killed, how miserable I should feel to have refused him and disappointed him—for the second time!"

"Wait a moment, Edith. Suppose, as you say, he goes out again and is killed, and you *haven't* disappointed him, what would your position be then?"

She couldn't answer.

"How is it your conscientiousness with regard to Bruce doesn't come in the way now? Why would it ruin him less now than formerly?"

"Bruce doesn't seem to matter so much."

"Because he isn't fighting?" asked Sir Tito.

"Oh no, Landi! I never thought of that. But you know he always imagines himself ill, and he's quite all right really. He'll enjoy his grievance. I *know* he won't be unhappy. And he's older, and he's not tied to that silly, mad girl he ran away with. And besides, I'm older. This is probably *my* last chance!"

She looked at Landi imploringly, as if begging his permission.

He answered calmly: "Écoute, chérie. When do you see him again?"

"I'm to take him for a drive tomorrow."

"My dear Edith, promise me one thing; don't undertake anything yet."

"But why not?"

"You mustn't. This may be merely an impulse; you may change again. It may be a passing mood."

"I don't think it is," said Edith. "Anyhow, it's my wish at present. It's the result of thinking, remember—not of his persuasion."

"Go for a drive, but give him no hope yet." He took both her hands. "Make no promise, except to me. Don't I know you well? I doubt if you could do it."

"Yes, I could! I could go through *anything* if I were determined, and if I had the children safe."

"Never mind that for the present. Live for the day. Will you promise me that?"

She hesitated for a moment.

Then he said:

"Really, dear, it's too serious to be impulsive about. Take time."

"Very well, Landi. I promise you that."

"Then we'll meet again afterwards and talk it over. I'll come and see you."

"Very well. And mustn't I tell him anything? Not make him a little bit happy?"

"Tell him nothing. Be nice to him. Enjoy your drive. Put off all decision at present."

He looked at her. Her eyes were sparkling, her colour, her expression were deepened. She looked all animation, with more life than he had ever seen in her. . . Somehow the sight made his heart ache a little, a very little.

Poor girl! Of course she had been starving for love, and hidden the longing under domestic interests, artistic, social, but human. But she deserved real love, a real lover. She was so loyal, so true herself.

"Tiens! You look like a lamp that has been lighted," said Sir Tito, chuckling a little to himself. "Eh, bien!—and the pretty nurse? Does she still dance the Cachuca? I know I'm old-fashioned, but it's impossible for me not to associate everything Spanish with the ridiculous. I think of guitars, mantillas, sombreros, or—what else is it? Ah, I know—onions."

"She isn't even Spanish, really!"

"Then why did you deceive me?" said Landi, a shade absently, with a glance at his watch and another in the mirror.

"She can't remain with Aylmer. She knows it herself. I'm trying to arrange for her to become a companion for Lady Conroy."

He laughed.

"You are more particular about her being chaperoned than you were last week."

"Landi, Aylmer will never care for her. She's a dear, but he won't."

"Tu ne l'a pas revu? Lui—Aylmer?"

"No, but he's written to me."

"Oh, for heaven's sake, my child, burn the letters! I daresay it won't be difficult; they are probably all flames already."

"I did have one lovely letter," said Edith.

She took it out of her dress. He glanced at it.

"Mon Dieu! To think that a pupil of mine drives about in a taxi-cab with compromising letters in her pocket! Non, tu est folle, véritablement, Edith."

To please him she threw it into the fire, after tearing a small blank piece of the paper off, and putting this unwritten-on scrap back in the bodice of her dress. As she hurried away, she again promised him not to undertake anything, nor to allow Aylmer to overpower her prudent intention during their drive.

"What time do you start? I think I shall come too," said Sir Tito, pretending to look at his engagement-book.

He burst out laughing at her expression.

"Ah, I'm not wanted! Tiens! If you're not very careful *one* person will go with you, I can tell you. And that will be Madame Frabelle."

"No, she won't. Indeed not! It's the last day of Archie's holidays."

"He's coming with you?"

"On the front seat, with the chauffeur," said Edith.

There was a ring at the bell. He lifted the curtain and caressingly but firmly pushed her through into the other room.

Sir Tito had another appointment.

XXII

While this drama was taking place in the little house in Sloane Street, Madame Frabelle, who lived for romance, and was always imagining it where it didn't exist, was, of course, sublimely unconscious of its presence. She had grown tired of her fancy about Edith and Mr. Mitchell, or she made herself believe that her influence had stopped it. But she was beginning to think, much as she enjoyed her visit and delighted in her surroundings, that it was almost time for her at least to *suggest* going away.

She had made Edith's friends her own. She was devoted to Edith, fonder of the children than anyone except their grandmother, and strangely, considering she was a visitor who gave trouble, she was adored by the servants and by everyone in the house, with the single exception of Archie.

She was carrying on a kind of half-religious flirtation with the Rev. Byrne Fraser, who was gradually succeeding in making her very high church. Sometimes she rose early and left the house mysteriously. She went to Mass. There was a dreamy expression in her eyes when she came back. A slight perfume of incense, instead of the lavender water that she formerly affected, was now observable about her.

She went to see the "London Group" and the "New English" with young Coniston, who explained to her all he had learnt from Aylmer, a little wrong; while she assured him that she knew nothing about pictures, but she knew what she liked.

She bought book-bindings from Miss Coniston, and showed her how to cook macaroni and how to make cheap but unpalatable soup for her brother. And she went to all the war concerts and bazaars got up by Valdez, to meetings for the Serbians arranged by Mrs. Mitchell and to Lady Conroy's Knitting Society for the Refugees. She was a very busy woman. But it was not these employments that were filling her mind as she sat in her own room, looking seriously at herself in the glass. Something made her a little preoccupied.

She was beginning to fear that Bruce was getting too fond of her.

The moment the idea occurred to her, it occurred to Bruce also. She had a hypnotic effect on him; as soon as she thought of anything he thought of it too. Something in her slight change of manner, her cautious way of answering, and of rustling self-consciously out of the room when they were left alone together, had this effect. Bruce was enchanted. Madame Frabelle thought he was getting too fond of her! Then, he must be! Perhaps he was. He certainly didn't like the idea at all of her going away and changed the subject directly she mentioned it. He had always thought her a very wonderful person. He was immensely impressed by her universal knowledge and agreeable manners and general charm. Still, Madame Frabelle was fifteen years older than Bruce, and Bruce himself was no chicken. Although he was under forty, his ideal of himself was that he liked only very young girls. This was not true. But as he thought it was, it became very much the same thing. As a matter of fact, only rather foolish girls were flattered at attentions from Bruce. Married women preferred spirited bachelors, and attractive girls preferred attractive boys. In fact, Bruce was not wanted socially, and he felt a little bit out of it among the men through not being among the fighters. The fact that he told everyone that he was not in khaki because he was in consumption didn't seem to make him more interesting to the general public. His neurotic heart bored his friends at the club. In fact there was not a woman, even his mother, except Madame Frabelle, who cared to listen to his symptoms. That she did so, and with sympathy, was one of her attractions.

But as long as she had listened to them in a sisterly, friendly way, he regarded her only as a friend—a friend of whom he was very proud, and whom he respected immensely. As has been said, she impressed him so much that he did not know she bored him. When she began rustling out of the room when they were left alone, and looking away, avoiding his eye when he stared at her absently, things were different, and he began to feel rather flattered. Of course it would be an infernal shame, and not the act of a gentleman, to take advantage of one's position as a host by making love to a fascinating guest. But there was so much sympathy between them! It is only fair to say that the idea would never have occurred to Bruce unless it had first occurred to Madame Frabelle. If a distinguished-looking woman in violet velvet leaves the room five minutes after she's left alone with one—even though she has grey hair— it naturally shows that she thinks one is dangerous. The result of it all was that when Bruce heard Edith was taking Aylmer for a drive, he apologised very much indeed for not going with her. He said, frankly, much as he liked Aylmer, wounded heroes were rather a bore. He hoped Aylmer would forgive him. And Madame Frabelle had promised to take him to the Oratory. She disapproved of his fancy of becoming a

Catholic; she was not one herself, though she was extremely high, and growing daily higher, but the music at the Oratory on that particular day was very wonderful, and they agreed to go there. And afterwards—well, afterwards they might stroll home, or—go and have tea in Bond Street.

IT WAS THE LAST DAY of Archie's holidays, and though it was rather cold his mother insisted on taking him with her.

Aylmer tried to hide the shade that came over his face when he saw the boy, but remembering that he had undertaken to be a father to him, he cheered up as soon as Archie was settled.

It was a lovely autumn day, one of those warm Indian-summer days that resemble early spring. There is the same suggestion of warmer sunshine yet to come; the air has a scent as of growing things, the kind of muffled hopes and suppressed excitement of April is in the deceptive air. This sort of day is dangerous to charming people not in their very first youth.

IN HIGH SPIRITS AND BEYOND the speed limit they started for Richmond.

XXIII

A week later Aylmer and his son were sitting looking at each other in the old brown library. Teddy had come over for ten days' leave from somewhere in France. Everyone, except his father, was astonished how little he had changed. He seemed exactly the same, although he had gone through strange experiences. But Aylmer saw a different look in his eyes. He looked well and brisk—perhaps a little more developed and more manly; his shoulders, always rather thick and broad, seemed even broader, although he was thinner. But it was the expression of the eyes that had altered. Those eyes had *seen things*. In colour pale blue, they had a slightly strained look. They seemed paler. His sunburn increased his resemblance to his father, always very striking. Both had large foreheads, clearly cut features and square chins. Aylmer was, strictly speaking, handsomer. His features more refined, more chiselled. But Teddy had the additional charm of extreme youth—youth with the self-possession and ease that seemed, as it were, a copy—as his voice was an echo—of his father. The difference was in culture and experience. Teddy had gone out when he was just on the point of going to Balliol, yet seemed to have something of the Oxford manner, characteristic of his father—a manner suave, amiable, a little ironical. He had the unmistakable public-school look and his training had immensely improved his appearance.

Aylmer was disappointed that the very first thing his son insisted on doing was to put on evening clothes and go to the Empire. That was where the difference in age told. Aylmer would not have gone to the Empire fresh from the fighting line. He made no objection, and concealed the tiniest ache that he felt when Teddy went out at once with Major Willis, an elder friend of his. Quite as old, Aylmer thought to himself, as *he* was. But not being a relative, he seemed of the same generation.

The next evening Teddy spent at home, and sat with his father, who declared himself to be completely recovered, but was still not allowed to put his foot to the ground, Miss Clay was asked to sing to them. Her voice, as has been said, was a very beautiful one, a clear, fine soprano, with a timbre rare in quality, and naturally thrilling. She had not been taught well enough to be a public success perhaps, but was much more accomplished than the average amateur.

Teddy delighted in it. She sang all the popular songs—she had a way that was almost humorous of putting refinement into the stupidest and vulgarest melody. And then she sang some of those technically poor but attaching melodies that, sung in a certain way, without sickening sentimentality or affectation, seem to search one's soul and bring out all that there is in one of romance.

She looked very beautiful, that Aylmer admitted to himself, and she sang simply and charmingly; that he owned also. Why did it irritate him so intensely to see Teddy moved and thrilled, to see his eyes brighten, his colour rise and to see him obviously admiring the girl? When she made an excuse to leave them Teddy was evidently quite disappointed.

The next day Aylmer limped down to the library. To his great surprise he heard voices in the room Dulcie used for her sitting-room. He heard Teddy begging her to sing to him again. He heard her refuse and then Teddy's voice asking her to go out to tea with him.

Aylmer limped as loudly as he could, and they evidently heard him, but didn't mind in the least. He didn't want Miss Clay to stop at home. He was expecting Edith.

"Hang it, let them go!" he said to himself, and he wondered at himself. Why should he care? Why *shouldn't* she flirt with the boy if she liked, or rather—for he was too just not to own that it was no desire of hers—why shouldn't the boy make up to her? Whatever the reason was, it annoyed him.

Annoyance was soon forgotten when Mrs. Ottley was announced.

Since their drive to Richmond there had been a period of extraordinary happiness and delight for Edith. Not another word had been said with reference to Aylmer's proposal. He left it in abeyance, for he saw to his great joy and delight that she was becoming her old self, more than her old self.

Edith was completely changed. The first thing she thought of now in the morning was how soon she should see him again. She managed to conceal it well, but she was nervous, absent, with her eyes always on the clock, counting the minutes. When other people were present she was cool and friendly to Aylmer, but when they were alone he had become intimate, delightful, familiar, like the time, three years ago, when they were together at the seaside. But her mother-in-law had then been in the house. And the children. Everything was so conventional. Now she was able to see him alone. Really alone. . . His eyes welcomed her as she came in. Having shut the door quietly, she reached his chair in a little rush.

"Don't take off your hat. I like that hat. That was the hat you wore the day I told you—"

"I'm glad it suits me," she said, interrupting. "Does it really? Isn't it too small?"

"You know it does."

He was holding her hand. He slowly took off the glove, saying: "What a funny woman you are, Edith. Why do you wear grey gloves? Nobody else wears grey gloves."

"I prefer white ones, but they won't stay white two minutes"

"I like these."

"Tell me about Teddy. Don't, Aylmer!"

Aylmer was kissing her fingers one by one. She drew them away.

"Teddy! Oh, there's not much to tell." Then he gave a little laugh. "I believe he's fallen in love with Miss Clay."

"Has he really? Well, no wonder; think how pretty she is."

"I know. Is she? I don't think she's a bit pretty."

"She's to see Lady Conroy tomorrow, you know," Edith said, divining an anxiety or annoyance in Aylmer on the subject.

"Yes. Will it be all right?"

"Oh yes."

"Well, Teddy's going back on Monday anyway, and I certainly don't need a nurse any more. Headley will do all I want."

Headley was the old butler.

"What scent do you use, Edith?"

"I hardly ever use any. I don't care for scent."

"But lately you have," he insisted. "What is it? I think I like it."

"It's got a silly name. It's called Omar Khayyám."

"I thought it was Oriental. I think you're Oriental, Edith. Though you're so fair and English-looking. How do you account for it?"

"I can't think," said Edith.

"Perhaps you're a fair Circassian," said he. "Do you think yourself you're Oriental?"

"I believe I am, in some ways. I like lying down on cushions. I like cigarettes, and scent, and flowers. I hate wine, and exercise, and cricket, and bridge."

"That isn't all that's needed. You wouldn't care for life in a harem, would you?" He laughed. "You with your independent mind and your cleverness."

"Perhaps not exactly, but I can imagine worse things."

"I shall take you to Egypt," he said. "You've never been there, have you?"

"Never." Her eyes sparkled.

"Yes, I shall take you to see the Sphinx. For the first time."

"Oh, you can't. You're looking very well, Aylmer, wonderfully better."

"I wonder why? You don't think I'm happy, do you?"

"I am," said Edith.

"Because you're a woman. You live for the moment. I'm anxious about the future."

"Oh, oh! You're quite wrong. It's not women who live for the moment," said Edith.

"No, I don't know that the average woman does. But then you're not an average woman."

"What am I?"

"You're Edith," he answered, rather fatuously. But she liked it. She moved away.

"Now that's awfully mean of you, taking advantage of my wounded limb."

She rang for tea.

"And that's even meaner. It's treacherous," he said, laughing.

She sat down on a chair at a little distance.

"Angel!" he said, in a low, distinct voice.

"It is not for me to dictate," said Edith, in a tone of command, "but I should think it more sensible of you not to say these things to me—just now."

The servant came in with tea.

XXIV

Just before Archie went back to school he made a remark that impressed Edith strangely. Quite dressed and ready to start, as he was putting on his gloves, he fell into one of his reveries. After being silent for some time he said:

"Mother!"

"Yes, darling?"

"Why doesn't father fight?"

"I told you before, darling. Your father is not very strong."

"Mother!"

"Yes, dear?"

"Is Aylmer older than father?"

"Yes. Aylmer's four years older. Why?"

"I don't know. I wish I had a father who could fight, like Aylmer. And I'd like to fight too, like Teddy."

"Aylmer hasn't any wife and children to leave. Teddy's eighteen; you're only ten."

"Mother!"

"Yes, dear?"

"I wish I was old enough to fight. And I wish father was stronger. . . Do you think I shall ever fight in this war?"

"Good heavens, dear! I hope it isn't going to last seven years more."

"I wish it would," said Archie ferociously. "Mother!"

"Yes, darling?"

"But what's the matter with father? He seems quite well."

"Oh, he isn't very well. He suffers from nerves."

"Nerves! What's nerves?"

"I think, darling, it's time for us to start. Where's your coat?"

She drove him to the station. Most of the way he was very silent As she put him in the train he said.

"Mother, give my love to Aylmer."

"All right, dear."

He then said:

"Mother, I wish Aylmer was my father."

"Oh, Archie! You mustn't say that."

But she never forgot the boy's remark. It had a stronger influence on her action later than anything else. She knew Archie had always had a great hero-worship for Aylmer. But that he should actually prefer him to Bruce!

She didn't tell Aylmer that for a long time afterwards.

Before returning to the front Teddy had become so violently devoted to Miss Clay that she was quite glad to see him go. She received his attentions with calm and cool friendliness, but gave him not the smallest encouragement. She was three years older, but looked younger than her age, while Teddy looked much older, more like twenty-two. So that when on the one or two occasions during his ten days' leave they went out together, they didn't seem at all an ill-assorted couple. And whenever Aylmer saw the two together, it created the greatest irritation in him. He hardly knew which vexed him more—Dulcie for being attractive to the boy, or the boy for being charmed by Dulcie. It was absurd—out of place. It displeased him.

A day or two after Teddy's departure Dulcie went to see Lady Conroy, who immediately declared that Dulcie was extraordinarily like a charming girl she had met at Boulogne. Dulcie convinced her that she was the same girl.

"Oh, how perfectly charming!" said Lady Conroy. "What a coincidence! *Too* wonderful! Well, my dear, I can see at a glance that you're the very person I want. Your duties will be very, *very* light. Oh, how light they will be! There's really hardly anything to do! I merely want you to be a sort of walking memorandum for me," Lady Conroy went on, smiling. "Just to recollect what day it is, and what's the date, and what time my appointments are, and do my telephoning for me, and write my letters, and take the dog out for a walk, and *sometimes* just hear my little girls practise, and keep my papers in order. Oh, one can hardly say exactly—you know the sort of thing. Oh yes! and do the flowers," said Lady Conroy, glancing round the room. "I always forget my flowers, and I won't let Marie do them, and so there they are—dead in the vases! And I do like a few live flowers about, I must say," she added pathetically.

Dulcie said she thought she could undertake it.

"Well, then, won't you stay now, and have your things sent straight on? Oh, do! I do wish you would. I've got two stalls for the St James's tonight. My husband can't come, and I can't think of anybody else to ask. I should love to take you."

Dulcie would have enjoyed to go. The theatre was a passion with her, as with most naïve people. She made some slight objection which Lady Conroy at once waved away. However, Dulcie pointed out that she must go home first, and as all terms and arrangements absolutely suited both parties, it was decided that Dulcie should go to the play with her tonight and come the next day to take up her duties.

She asked Lady Conroy if she might have her meals alone when there were guests, as she was very shy. A charming little sitting-room, opening out of the drawing-rooms, was put at her disposal.

"Oh, certainly, dear; always, of course, except when I'm alone. But you'll come when I ask you, now and then, won't you? I thought you'd be very useful sometimes at boring lunches, or when there were too many men—that sort of thing. And I hear you sing. Oh, that will be delightful! You'll sing when we have a few tedious people with us? I adore music. We'll go to some of those all-British concerts, won't we? We must be patriotic. Do you know it's really been my dream to have a sweet, useful, sympathetic girl in the house. And with a memory too! Charming!"

Dulcie went away fascinated, if slightly bewildered. It was a pang to her to say good-bye to Aylmer, the more so as he showed, in a way that was perfectly obvious to the girl, that he was pleased to see her go, though he was as cordial as possible.

She had been an embarrassment to him of late. It was beginning to be what is known as a false position, since Headley the butler could now look after Aylmer. Except for a limp, he was practically well.

Anyone who has ever nursed a person to whom they are devoted, helped him through weakness and danger to health again, will understand the curious pain she felt to see him independent of her, anxious to show his strength. Still, he had been perfect. She would always remember him with worship. She meant never to love anyone else all her life.

When she said good-bye she said to him:

"I do hope you'll be very happy."

He laughed, coloured a little, and said as he squeezed her hand warmly:

"You've been a brick to me, Miss Clay. I shall certainly tell you if I ever am happy."

She wondered what that meant, but she preferred to try to forget it.

ADA LEVERSON

When Dulcie arrived, as she had been told, at a quarter to eight, dressed in a black evening dress (she didn't care to wear uniform at the theatre), she found Lady Conroy, who was lying on the sofa in a tea-gown, utterly astonished to see her.

"My dear! you've come to dine with me after all?"

"No, indeed. I've dined. You said I was to come in time to go to the play."

"The play? Oh! I forgot. I'm so sorry. I've sent the tickets away. I forgot I'd anyone to go with me. I'm afraid it can't be helped now. Are you very disappointed? Poor child. Well, dear, you'll dine with me, anyhow, as you've come, and I can tell you all about what we shall have to do, and everything. We'll go to the theatre some other evening."

Dulcie was obliged to decline eating two dinners. She had not found it possible to get through one—her last meal at Aylmer's house. However, as she had no idea what else to do, she remained with Lady Conroy. And she spent a very pleasant evening.

Lady Conroy told her all about herself, her husband, her children and her friends. She told her the history of her life, occasionally branching off on to other subjects, and referring to the angel she had met on a boat who was in the Black Watch, and who, Dulcie gathered, was a wounded officer. Lady Conroy described all the dresses she had at present, many that she had had in former years, and others that she would like to have had now. She gravely told the girl the most inaccurate gossip about such of her friends as Dulcie might possibly meet later. She was confidential, amusing, brilliant and inconsequent. She appeared enchanted with Dulcie, whom she treated like an intimate friend at sight. And Dulcie was charmed with her, though somewhat confused at her curious memory. Indeed, they parted at about eleven the best possible friends; Lady Conroy insisting on sending her home in her car.

Dulcie, who had a sensitive and sensible horror of snobbishness, felt sorry to know that her father would casually mention that his daughter was staying with the Conroys in Carlton House Terrace, and that her stepmother would scold her unless she recollected every dress she happened to see there. Still, on the whole she felt cheered.

She had every reason to hope that she would be as happy as a companion, in love without hope of a return, could be under any circumstances.

XXV

Madame Frabelle and Edith were sitting side by side in Edith's boudoir. Madame Frabelle was knitting. Edith was looking at a book. It was a thin little volume of essays, bound by Miss Coniston.

"What is the meaning of this design?" Edith said. "It seems to me very unsuited to Chesterton's work! Olive-green, with twirly things on it!"

"I thought it rather artistic," answered Madame Frabelle.

"It looks like macaroni, or spaghetti. Perhaps the idea was suggested by your showing her how to cook it," said Edith, laughing.

Madame Frabelle looked gravely serene.

"No—I don't think that had anything to do with it."

"How literal you are, Eglantine!"

"Am I? I think you do me injustice, Edith dear," returned the amiable guest with a tinge of stateliness as she rolled up her wool.

Edith smiled, put down her book, looked at the clock and rearranged the large orange-coloured cushion behind her back. Then she took the book up again, looked through it and again put it down.

"You're not at all—forgive me for saying so—not the least bit in the world restless today, Edith darling, are you?" said Madame Frabelle in a calm, clear, high voice that Edith found quite trying.

"Oh, I hope not—I think not."

"Ah, that's well," and Madame Frabelle, with one slight glance at her hostess, went on knitting.

"I believe I miss Archie a good deal," said Edith.

"Ah, yes, you must indeed. I miss the dear boy immensely myself," sympathetically said Madame Frabelle. But Edith thought Madame Frabelle bore his loss with a good deal of equanimity, and she owned to herself that it was not surprising. The lady had been very good to Archie, but he had teased her a good deal. Like the Boy Scouts, but the other way round, he had almost made a point of worrying her in some way or other every day. Edith could never persuade him to change his view of her.

He said she was a fool.

Somehow, today Edith felt rather pleased with him for thinking so. All women are subject to moods, particularly, perhaps, those who have a visitor staying with them for a considerable time. There are moments of injustice, of unfairness to the most charming feminine guest, from the most gentle hostess. And also there are, undoubtedly, times when the nicest hostess gets a little on one's nerves.

So—critical, highly strung—Madame Frabelle was feeling today. So was Edith. Madame Frabelle was privately thinking that Edith was restless, that she had lost her repose, that her lips were redder than they used to be. Had she taken to using lip salve too? She was inclined to smile, with a twinkle in her eye, at Madame Frabelle's remarks, a shade too often. And what was Edith thinking of at this moment? She was thinking of Archie's remarks about Madame Frabelle. That boy had genius!

But there would be a reaction, probably during, or immediately after, tea-time, for these two women were sincerely fond of one another. The irritating fact that Edith was eighteen years younger than her guest made Eglantine feel sometimes a desire to guide, even to direct her, and if she had the disadvantage in age she wanted at least the privilege of gratifying her longing to give advice.

The desire became too strong to be resisted. The advantage of having something to do with her hands while she spoke was too great a one not to be taken advantage of. So Madame Frabelle said:

"Edith dear."

"Yes?"

"I've been wanting to say something to you."

Edith leant forward, putting her elbows on her knees and her face on her hands, and said:

"Oh, *do* tell me, Eglantine. What is it?"

"It is simply this," said the other lady, calmly continuing her knitting. . . "Very often when one's living with a person, one doesn't notice little things a comparative stranger would observe. Is that not so?"

"What have you observed? What's it about?"

"It is about your husband," said Madame Frabelle.

"What! Bruce?" asked Edith.

"Naturally," replied Madame Frabelle dryly.

"What have you observed about Bruce?"

"I have observed," replied Madame Frabelle, putting her hand in the sock that she was knitting, and looking at it critically, her head on one side, "I have observed that Bruce is not at all well."

"Oh, I'm sorry you think that. It's true he has seemed rather what he calls off colour lately."

"He suffers," said Madame Frabelle, as if announcing a great discovery, "he suffers from Nerves."

"I know he does, my dear. Who should know it better than I do? But—do you think he is worse lately?"

"I do. He is terribly depressed. He says things to me sometimes that—well, that really quite alarm me."

"I'm sorry. But you mustn't take Bruce too seriously, you know that."

"Indeed I don't take him too seriously! And I've done my best either to change the subject or to make him see the silver lining to every cloud," Madame Frabelle answered solemnly, with a shake of her head.

"I think what Bruce complains of is the want of a silver lining to his purse," Edith said.

"You are jesting, Edith dear."

"No, I'm not. He worries about money."

"But only incidentally," said Madame Frabelle. "Bruce is really worried about the war."

"Naturally. But surely—I suppose we all are."

"But Mr. Ottley takes it particularly to heart," said Madame Frabelle, with a kind of touching dignity.

Edith looked at her in a little surprise. Why did she suddenly call Bruce "your husband" or "Mr. Ottley"?

"Why this distant manner, Eglantine?" said Edith, half laughing. "I thought you always called him Bruce."

"I beg your pardon; yes, I forgot. Well, don't you see, Edith dear, that what we might call his depression, his melancholy point of view, is—is growing worse and worse?"

Edith got up, walked to the other end of the room, rearranged some violets in a copper vase and came back to the sofa again. Madame Frabelle followed her with her eyes. Then Edith said, picking up the knitting:

"Take care, dear, you're losing your wool. Yes; perhaps he is worse. He might be better if he occupied his mind more."

"He works at the Foreign Office from ten till four every day," said Madame Frabelle in a tone of defence; "he looks in at his club, where they talk over the news of the war, and then he comes home and we discuss it again. . . Really, Edith, I scarcely see how much more he could do!"

"Oh, my dear, but don't you see all the time he doesn't do anything?—anything about the war, I mean. Now both you and I do our little best to help, in one way or another. You especially, I'm sure, do a tremendous lot; but what does Bruce do? Nothing, except talk."

"That's just it, Edith. I doubt if your husband is in a fit state of health to strain his mind by any more work than he does already. He's not strong, dear; remember that."

"Of course, I know; if he were all right he wouldn't be here," said Edith. "I suppose he really does suffer a great deal."

"What was it again that prevented him joining?" asked Madame Frabelle, with sympathetic tenderness.

"Neurotic heart," answered Edith. Though she tried her very utmost she could not help the tone of her voice sounding a little dry and ironical. Of course, she did not in the least believe in Bruce's neurotic heart, but she did not want Madame Frabelle to know that.

"Ah! ah! that must cause him a great deal of pain, but I think so far his worst symptoms are his nervous fears. Look at last night," continued Madame Frabelle, and now she put down her knitting and folded it into her work-basket." Last night, because there was no moon, and it wasn't raining, and fairly clear, Mr. Ott—Bruce had absolutely made up his mind there would be a Zeppelin raid. It was his own idea."

"Not quite, dear. Young Coniston, who is a special constable, rang up and told him that there was a chance of the Zeppelins last night."

"Well, perhaps so. At any rate he believed it. Well, instead of being satisfied when I told him that I had got out my mask, that I saw to the bath being left half-filled with water, helped your husband to put two large bags of sand outside his dressing-room—in spite of all that, do you know what happened in the middle of the night?"

"I'm afraid I don't," said Edith. "Since Archie went back to school I have had Dilly in my room, and we both slept soundly all night."

"Did you? I fancied I saw a light in your room."

This was quite true. Edith was writing a very long letter.

"Ah, perhaps."

"Well, at three o'clock in the morning, fancy my surprise to hear a knock at my door!"

"I wonder I didn't hear a knock at mine," said Edith.

"Your husband was afraid to disturb the little girl. Most considerate, I thought. Well, he knocked at my door and said that he was unable to sleep, that he felt terribly miserable and melancholy, in fact was wretched, and that he felt on the point of cutting his throat. . . Don't be frightened, dear. I don't mean that he really *meant* it," said Madame Frabelle, putting her hand on Edith's.

"Poor fellow! But what a shame to disturb you."

"I didn't mind in the least. I was only too pleased. Well, what do you think I did? I got up and dressed, went down to the library and lighted the fire, and sat up for half-an-hour with your husband trying to cheer him up!"

"Did you really?" Edith smiled. "It was very sweet of you, Eglantine."

"Not at all; I was only too glad. I made a cup of tea, Bruce had a whisky and soda, we had a nice talk, and I sent him back quite cheerful. Still, it just shows, doesn't it, how terribly he takes it all?"

"Rather hard on you, Eglantine; quite improper too," laughed Edith as she rang the bell.

Madame Frabelle ignored this remark.

"If I could only feel at all that I've done a little good during my stay here, I shall be quite satisfied."

"Oh! but you mustn't dream yet of—" began Edith.

There was a ring at the bell.

"Why, here is Bruce, just in time for tea."

Edith went to meet him in the hall. Although he came in with his key, he invariably rang the bell, so that the maid could take his coat and stick.

"Hallo, Edith," he said, in a rather sober tone. "How are you? And where is Madame Frabelle?"

XXVI

B ruce came in with a rather weary air, and sat down by the fire. Madame Frabelle was presiding at the tea-table.

"How are you feeling, Bruce?" Edith asked.

"Oh, pretty rotten. I had a very bad night. How are you, Madame Frabelle?"

"Oh, very well. Tea?"

"Poor Bruce!" said Edith kindly. "Oh, and poor Madame Frabelle," she added, with a smile.

Bruce gave Madame Frabelle a slightly reproachful look as he took a cup of tea from her.

"I've been telling Edith," said that lady in a quiet, dignified way.

"What about?"

"About last night," said Madame Frabelle, passing Bruce the buttered toast without looking at him, as if avoiding his glance.

"I'm really very much ashamed of it," said Bruce. "You can't think how kind she was to me, Edith."

"I'm sure she was," said Edith.

"Oh, you won't have a bad night like that again," said Madame Frabelle cheerily.

"I'm sure I hope not." He gave a dark, despairing look, and sighed. "Upon my word, if it hadn't been for her I don't know what I would have done." He shook his head and stroked his back hair.

Suddenly Edith felt intensely bored. Madame Frabelle and Bruce were looking at each other with such intense sympathy, and she knew they would repeat in different words what they had said already. They were so certain to go over the same ground again and again! . . . Edith felt she was not wanted. But that didn't annoy her. She was merely thinking of an excuse to get away from them.

"By the way, how's Aylmer, Edith?" asked Bruce.

"Getting on well. I believe he's been ordered out of town."

"To the seaside? For God's sake don't let him go to the east coast!"

"The east coast is quite as safe as any other part of England, *I* think." said Madame Frabelle.

"Oh, he'll take his chance," Edith replied.

"I expect he'll miss *you*, my dear," said Bruce. "You've been so jolly good to him lately."

"Naturally," said Madame Frabelle, a little quickly, very smoothly, and with what Edith thought unnecessary tact. "Naturally. Anyone so kind-hearted as Edith would be sure to try and cheer up the convalescence of a wounded friend. Have a *foie-gras* sandwich, Edith?"

Edith felt an almost irresistible desire to laugh at something in the hospitable, almost patronising tone of her guest.

"Oh, Edith likes going to see him," said Bruce to Madame Frabelle. "So do I, if it comes to that. We're all fond of old Aylmer, you know."

"I know. I quite understand. You're great friends. Personally, I think Mr. Ross has behaved splendidly." Madame Frabelle said this with an air of self-control and scrupulous justice.

"You don't care very much about him, I fancy," said Bruce with the air of having made a subtle discovery.

She raised one eyebrow slightly. "I won't say that. I see very excellent points in him. I admit there's a certain coldness, a certain hard reserve about his character that—Well, frankly, it doesn't appeal to me. But I hope I am fair to him. He's a man I respect. . . Yes, I respect him."

"But he doesn't amuse you—what?" said Bruce.

"The fact is, he has no sense of humour," said Madame Frabelle.

"Fancy your finding that out now!" said Bruce, with a broad smile. "Funny! Ha ha! Very funny! Do you know, it never occurred to me! But now I come to think of it—yes, perhaps that's what's the matter with him. Mind you, I call him a jolly, cheery sort of chap. Quite an optimist—a distinct optimist. You never find Aylmer depressed."

"No, not depressed. It isn't that. But he hasn't got—You won't either of you be angry with me for what I say, will you?"

"Oh no, indeed."

"You won't be cross with me, Edith? Perhaps I ought not to say it."

"Yes, do tell us," urged Edith.

"Well, what I consider is the defect in Aylmer Ross is that he has brains, but no temperament."

"Excellent!" cried Bruce. "Perfectly true. Temperament! That's what he wants!"

Edith remembered hearing that phrase used in her presence to Madame Frabelle—not about Aylmer, but about someone else. It was very characteristic of Madame Frabelle to catch up an idea or a phrase, misapply it, and then firmly regard it as her own.

Bruce shook his head. "Brains, but no temperament! Excellent!"

"Mind you, that doesn't prevent him being an excellent soldier," went on Madame Frabelle.

"Oh dear, no. He's done jolly well," said Bruce. "I think I know what she means—don't you, Edith?"

"I'm sure *she* does," said Edith, who had her doubts. "I don't know that I do quite know what people mean when they say other people haven't got temperament. The question is—what *is* temperament?"

"Oh, my dear, it's a sort of—a something—an atmosphere—a sympathy. What I might call the magnetism of personality!"

"That's right!" said Bruce, passing his cup for another cup of tea. "Aylmer's hard, hard as nails."

"Hasn't he got the name of being rather warm-hearted and impulsive, though?" suggested Edith.

"Oh, he's good-natured enough," said Bruce. "Very generous. I've known him to do ever so many kind things and never let a soul except the fellow he'd helped know anything about it."

"You don't understand me," said Madame Frabelle. "I don't doubt that for a moment. He's a generous man, because he has a sense of duty and of the claims of others. But he has the effect on me—"

"Go on, Eglantine."

"Frankly, he chills me," said Madame Frabelle. "When I went to see him with Edith, I felt more tired after a quarter of an hour's talk with him than I would—" She glanced at Bruce.

"Than you would after hours with Landi, or Bruce, or Byrne Fraser, or young Coniston," suggested Edith.

"That's what I mean. He's difficult to talk to."

"I have no doubt you're right," said Edith.

"Well, she generally is," said Bruce. "The only thing is she's so infernally deep sometimes, she sees things in people that nobody else would suspect. Oh, you do, you know!"

"Oh, do I?" said Madame Frabelle modestly.

"Yes, I think you do," said Edith, who by this time felt inclined to throw the tea-tray at her guest. The last fortnight Edith's nerves had certainly not been quite calm. Formerly she would have been amused at the stupidity of the conversation. Now she felt irritated, bored and worried, except when she was with Aylmer.

There was a moment's silence. Bruce leant back and half shut his eyes. Madame Frabelle softly put a cushion behind his shoulder, putting a finger on her lip as she looked at Edith.

Edith suddenly got up.

"You won't think it horrid of me, Bruce? I've got to go out for a few minutes."

"Oh no, no, no!" said Bruce. "Certainly not. Do go, my dear girl. You'll be back to dinner?"

"Dinner? Of course. It isn't a quarter to six."

Her eyes were bright. She looked full of elasticity and spirit again.

"I quite forgot," she said, "something that I promised to do for Mrs. Mitchell. And she'll be disappointed if I don't."

"I know what it is," said Madame Frabelle archly. "It's about that Society for the Belgians,"—she lowered her voice—"I mean the children's *lingerie*!"

"That's it," said Edith gratefully. "Well, I'll fly—and be back as soon as I can."

Bruce got up and opened the door for her.

"For heaven's sake don't treat me with ceremony, my dear Edith," said Madame Frabelle.

She made a little sign, as much as to say that she would look after Bruce. But she was not very successful in expressing anything by a look or a gesture. Edith had no idea what she meant. However, she nodded in return, as if she fully comprehended, and then ran up to her room, put on her hat, and, too impatient to wait while the servant called a cab, walked as quickly as possible until she met one near the top of Sloane Street. It was already very dark.

"Twenty-seven Jermyn Street," said Edith as she jumped in.

TEN MINUTES LATER SHE WAS sitting next to Aylmer.

"Only for a second; I felt I must see you."

"Fool! Angel!" said Aylmer, beaming, and kissing her hand.

"Bruce is too irritating for words today. And Madame Frabelle makes me sick. I can't stand her. At least today."

"Oh, Edith, don't tell me you're jealous of the woman! I won't stand it! I shan't play."

"Good heavens, no! Not in the least. But her society's so tedious at times. She has such a pompous way of discovering the obvious."

"I do believe you object to her being in love with Bruce," said Aylmer reproachfully. "That's a thing I will *not* stand."

"Indeed I don't. Besides, she's not. Who could be? . . . And don't be jealous of Bruce, Aylmer. . . I know she's very motherly to him, and kind. But she's the same to everyone."

They talked on for a few minutes. Then Edith said:

"Good-bye. I must go."

"Good-bye," said Aylmer.

"Oh! Are you going to let me go already?" she asked reproachfully.

She leant over him. Some impulse seemed to draw her near to him.

"You're using that Omar Khayyám scent again," he said. "I wish you wouldn't."

"Why? you said you liked it."

"I do like it. I like it too much."

She came nearer. Aylmer gently pushed her away.

"How unkind you are!" she said, colouring a little with hurt feeling.

"I can't do that sort of thing," said Aylmer in a low voice. "When once you've given me your promise—but not before."

"Oh, Aylmer!"

"I won't rush you. You'll see I'm right in time, dear girl."

"You don't love me!" suddenly exclaimed Edith.

"But that's where you're wrong. I do love you. And I wish you'd go."

She looked into his eyes, and then said, looking away:

"Are you really going out of town?"

"I'm ordered to. But I doubt if I can stand it."

"Well, good-bye, Aylmer dear."

"Fiend! Are you going already? Cruel girl!"

"Why you've just sent me away!"

"I can stand talking to you, Edith. Talking, for hours. But I can't stand your being within a yard of me."

"Thank you so much," she said, laughing, and arranging her hat in front of the mirror.

He spoke in a lower voice:

"How often must I tell you? You know perfectly well."

"What?"

"I'm not that sort of man."

"What sort?"

After a moment's pause he said:

"I can't kiss people."

"I'm very glad you can't. I have no wish for you to kiss *people*."

"I can't kiss. I don't know how anyone can. I can't do those things."

She pretended not to hear, looked round the room, took up a book and said:

"Will you lend me this, Aylmer?"

"No, I'll give it you."

"Good-bye."

"Good-bye, darling," said Aylmer, ringing the bell.

The butler called her a cab, and she drove to Mrs. Mitchell's.

When she got to the door she left a message with the footman to say she hadn't been able to see about that matter for Mrs. Mitchell yet, but would do it tomorrow.

Just as she was speaking Mr. Mitchell came up to the door.

"Hallo, hallo, hallo!" he cried in his cheery, booming voice.

"Hallo, Edith! How's Bruce?"

"Why, you ought to know. He's been with you today," said Edith.

"He seems a bit off colour at the Foreign Office. Won't you all three come and dine with us tomorrow? No party. I'm going to ring up and get Aylmer. It won't hurt him to dine quietly with us."

"We shall be delighted," said Edith.

Mr. Mitchell didn't like to see her go, but as he was longing to tell his wife a hundred things that interested them both, he waved his hand to her, saying:

"Good-bye. The war will be over in six months. Mark my words! And then won't we have a good time!"

"Dear Mr. Mitchell!" said Edith to herself as she drove back home in the dark.

XXVII

Landi was growing rather anxious about his favourite, for it was quite obvious to him that she was daily becoming more and more under the spell. Curious that the first time she should have found the courage to refuse, and that now, after three years' absence and with nothing to complain of particularly on the subject of her husband, she should now be so carried away by this love.

She had developed, no doubt. She was touched also, deeply moved at the long fidelity Aylmer had shown. He was now no longer an impulsive admirer, but a devotee. Even that, however, would not have induced her to think of making such a break in her life if it hadn't been for the war. Yes, Sir Tito put it all down to the war. It had an exciting, thrilling effect on people. It made them reckless. When a woman knows that the man she loves has risked his life, and is only too anxious to risk it again— well, it's natural that she should feel she is also willing to risk something. Valour has always been rewarded by beauty. And then her great sense of responsibility, her conscientiousness about Bruce—no wonder that had been undermined by his own weak conduct. How could Edith help feeling a slight contempt for a husband who not only wouldn't take any chances while he was still within the age, but positively imagined himself ill. True, Bruce had always been a *malade imaginaire*; like many others with the same weakness, his valetudinarianism had been terribly increased by the anxiety and worry of the war. But there was not much sympathy about for it just now. While so much real suffering was going on, imaginary ills were ignored, despised or forgotten.

Bruce hated the war; but he didn't hate it for the sake of other people so much as for his own. The interest that the world took in it positively bored him—absurd as it seems to say so, Edith was convinced that he was positively jealous of the general interest in it! He had great fear of losing his money, a great terror of Zeppelins; he gave way to his nerves instead of trying to control them. Edith knew his greatest wish would have been, had it been possible, to get right away from everything and go and live in Spain or America, or somewhere where he could hear no more about the war. Such a point of view might be understood in the case, say, of a great poet, a great artist, a man of genius, without any feeling of patriotism, or even a man beyond the age; but Bruce—he was the most ordinary and average of human beings, the most commonplace

Englishman of thirty-seven who had ever been born; that Bruce should feel like that did seem to Edith a little—contemptible; yet she was sorry for him, she knew he really suffered from insomnia and nerves, though he looked a fine man and had always been regarded as a fair sportsman. He had been fair at football and cricket, and could row a bit, and was an enthusiastic golfist; still, Edith knew he would never have made a soldier. Bruce wanted to be wrapped up in cotton wool, petted, humoured, looked up to and generally spoilt.

BUT WHAT SIR TITO FELT most was the thought of his favourite, who had forgiven her husband that escapade three years ago, now appearing in an unfavourable light. She had been absolutely faithful to Bruce in every way, under many temptations, and he knew she was still absolutely faithful. Aylmer and Edith were neither of them the people for secret meetings, for deception. It was not in her to *tromper* her husband while pretending to be a devoted wife, and it was equally unlike Aylmer to be a false friend.

Landi was too much of a man of the world to have been particularly shocked, even if he had known they had both deceived Bruce. Privately, for Edith's own sake he almost wished they had. He hated scandal to touch her; he thought she would feel it more than she supposed. But, after all, he reflected, had they begun in that way it would have been sure to end in an elopement, with a man of Aylmer's spirit and determination. Aylmer, besides, was far too exclusive in his affections, far too jealous, ever to be able to endure to see Edith under Bruce's thumb, ordered about, trying to please him; and indeed Landi was most anxious that they should not be alone too much, in case, now that Edith cared for him so much, his feelings would carry him away. . . Yes, if it once went too far the elopement was a certainty.

Would the world blame her so very much? That Bruce would let her take the children Landi had no doubt. He would never stand the bother of them; he wouldn't desire the responsibility; his pride might be a little hurt, but on the whole Sir Tito shrewdly suspected, as did Edith herself, that there would be a certain feeling of relief. Bruce had become such an egotist that, though he would miss Edith's devotion, he wouldn't grudge her the care of the children. Aylmer had pledged her his faith, his whole future; undoubtedly he would marry her and take the children as his own; still, Edith would bear the brunt before the world.

ADA LEVERSON

This Sir Tito did not fancy at all, and instinctively he began to watch Bruce. He felt very doubtful of him. The man who had flirted with the governess, who had eloped with the art student—was it at all likely that he was utterly faithful to Edith now? It was most unlikely. And Edith's old friend hoped that things would be adjusted in fairness to her.

He knew she would be happy with Aylmer. Why should she not at thirty-five begin a new life with the man she really cared for—a splendid fellow, a man with a fine character, with all his faults, who felt the claims of others, who had brains, pluck, and a sense of honour?

But Aylmer was going out again to the front. Until he returned again, nothing should be done. They should be patient.

XXVIII

Dulcie had now been settled down with Lady Conroy for about a week. She found her luxurious life at Carlton House Terrace far more congenial than she had expected. Her own orderly ways were obviously a great comfort to her employer, and though Lady Conroy turned everything to chaos as soon as Dulcie had put it straight, still she certainly had a good effect on things in general. She had a charming sitting-room to herself, and though she sometimes sighed for the little Chippendale room with the chintzes, at Jermyn Street, she was on the whole very contented. Lady Conroy was a delightful companion. She seldom pressed Dulcie to come down to meals when there were guests. Occasionally she did so, but so far the only person Dulcie had met more than once was Valdez, the handsome composer, who was trying so hard, with the help of Lady Conroy and his War Emergency Concerts, to assist such poor musicians as were suffering from the war, and at the same time to assert the value of British music.

Dulcie had been immensely struck by the commanding appearance and manner of Valdez, known everywhere as a singer, a writer of operas and a favourite of foreign royalties.

Landi she had often met at Aylmer's, but, privately, she was far more impressed by Valdez; first, he was English, though, like herself, of Spanish descent, and then he had none of the *méchanceté* and teasing wit that made her uncomfortable with Landi. He treated her with particularly marked courtesy, and he admired her voice, for Lady Conroy had good-naturedly insisted on her singing to him. He had even offered, when he had more time, to give her a few lessons. Lady Conroy told her a hundred interesting stories about him and Dulcie found a tinge of romance about him that helped to give piquancy to her present life.

Dulcie was very much afraid of Lord Conroy, though he didn't appear to notice her. In his own way he was as absent-minded as his wife, to whom he was devoted, but whose existence was entirely independent of his.

Lord Conroy had his own library, his own secretary, his own suite of rooms, his own motor, he didn't even tell his wife when he intended to dine out, and if he occasionally spoke to her of the strained political situation which now absorbed him, it certainly wasn't when Dulcie was there. With his grey beard and dark, eyebrows, and absent, distinguished manner, he was exactly what Dulcie would have dreamed of as an ideal Cabinet Minister. He evidently regarded his wife, despite her thirty-eight years and plumpness, almost as a child, giving her complete freedom to pursue her own devices, admiring her appearance, and smiling at her lively and inconsequent conversation; he didn't seem to take her seriously. Dulcie was particularly struck by the fact that they each had their own completely distinct circle of friends, and except when they gave a party or a large dinner these friends hardly met, and certainly didn't clash.

As everyone in the house had breakfasts independently, and as Dulcie didn't even dine downstairs unless Lady Conroy was alone, she saw very little of the man whom she knew to be a political celebrity, and whose name was on almost everybody's lips just now. She heard from his wife that he was worried and anxious, and hoped the war wouldn't last much longer.

There were no less than seven children, from the age of twelve downwards. Two of these lived in the schoolroom with the governess, one boy was at school, and the rest lived in the nursery with the nurse. One might say there were five different sets of people living different lives in different rooms, in this enormous house. Sometimes Dulcie thought it was hardly quite her idea of home life, a thing Lady Conroy talked of continually with great sentiment and enthusiasm, but it was pleasant enough. Since she was here to remember engagements and dates everything seemed to go on wheels.

One day, feeling very contented and in good spirits, she had gone to see her father with an impulse to tell him how well she was getting on. Directly the door was opened by the untidy servant Dulcie felt that something had happened, that some blow had fallen. Everything looked different. She found her father in his den surrounded by papers, his appearance and manner so altered that the first thing she said was:

"Oh, papa! what's the matter?"

Her father looked up. At his expression she flew to him and threw her arms round him. Then, of course, he broke down. Strange that with all women and most men it is only genuine sympathy that makes them give way. With a cool man of the world, or with a hard, cold, heartless daughter who had reproached him, Mr. Clay would have been as casual as an undergraduate.

At her sweetness he lost his self-control, and then he told her everything.

It was a short, commonplace, second-rate story, quite trivial and middle-class, and *how* tragic! He had gambled, played cards, lost, then fallen back on the resource of the ill-judged and independent-minded—gone to the professional lenders. Mr. Clay was not the sort of man who would ever become a sponge, a nuisance to friends. He was far too proud, and though he had often helped other people, he had never yet asked for help. In a word, the poor little house was practically in ruins, or rather, as he explained frankly enough (giving all details), unless he could get eighty pounds by the next morning his furniture would be sold and he and his wife would be turned out. Mr. Clay had a great horror of a smash. He was imprudent, even reckless, but had the sense of honour that would cause him to suffer acutely, as Dulcie knew. Of course she offered to help; surely since she had three hundred a year of her own she could do something, and he had about the same. . . The father explained that he had already sold his income in advance. And her own legacy had been left so that she was barred from anticipation. Dulcie, who was practical enough, saw that her own tiny income was absolutely all that the three would have to live on until her father got something else, and that bankruptcy was inevitable unless she could get him eighty pounds in a day.

"It's so little," he said pathetically, "and just to think that if Blue Boy hadn't been scratched I should have been bound to—Well, well, I know. I'm not going to bet any more."

She made him promise to buck up, she would consult her friends. . . Lady Conroy would perhaps be angelic and advance her her salary. (Of course she loathed the idea when she had been there only a week of being a nuisance and—But she must try.) It was worth anything to see her father brighten up. He told her to go and see her stepmother.

Mrs. Clay received her with the tenderest expressions and poured out her despairs and her troubles; she also confided in Dulcie that she had some debts that her husband knew nothing of and must *never* know. If only Dulcie could manage to get her thirty pounds—surely it would be easy enough with all her rich friends!—it would save her life. Dulcie promised to try, but begged her not to bother so much about dress in future.

"Of course I won't, darling! You're a pet and an angel. *Darling* Dulcie!

The truth is I adore your father. And he always told me that he fell in love with me because I looked so smart! I was so terrified of losing his affection by getting dowdy, don't you see? Besides, he doesn't take the slightest notice what I wear, he never knows what I've got on! Always betting or absorbed in the Racing Intelligence; it's really dreadful."

Dulcie promised anything, at least to do her best, if only Mrs. Clay would be kind, sweet to her father.

"Don't scold him, don't reproach him," she begged. "I'm sure he'll be terribly ill unless you're very patient and sweet to him. And I promise he shall never know about your debts."

Mrs. Clay looked at her in wonder and gratitude. The real reason Dulcie took on herself the wife's separate troubles and resolved to keep them from her father was that she felt sure that if he reproached his wife she would retort and then there would be a miserable state of feud in the house, where at least there had been peace and affection till now. Dulcie couldn't endure the idea of her father being made unhappy, and she thought that by making her stepmother under an obligation to her, she would have a sort of hold or influence and could make her behave well and kindly to her husband. Dulcie hadn't the slightest idea how she was going to do it, but she would.

She never even thought twice about giving up her income to her father. She was only too delighted to be able to do it. And she believed that his pride and sense of honour might really even make him stop gambling. And then there was some chance of happiness for the couple again.

DULCIE HAD REALLY UNDERTAKEN MORE of a sacrifice for her stepmother, whom she rather disliked, than for her father, whom she adored, but it was for his sake. She left them cheered, grateful, and relying on her.

WHEN SHE GOT HOME TO her charming room at Carlton House Terrace she sat down, put her head in her hands and began to think. She had undertaken to get a hundred and ten pounds in two days.

How was she to do it? Of course she knew that Aylmer Ross would be able and willing, indeed enchanted, to come to the rescue. He was always telling her that she had saved his life.

She would like to get his sympathy and interest, to remind him of her existence.

But she was far too much in love with him still to endure the thought of a request for money—that cold douche on friendship! She would rather go to anyone in the world than Aylmer.

What about Edith Ottley? Edith had been kindness itself to her; it was entirely through Edith that she had this position as secretary and companion at a salary of a hundred a year which now would mean so much to her.

She admired Edith more than any woman she knew; she thought her lovely, elegant, clever, fascinating and kindness itself. Yet she would dislike to ask Edith even more than Aylmer. The reason was obvious. Edith was her rival. Of course it was not her fault. She had not taken Aylmer away from her, she was his old friend, but the fact remained that her idol was in love with Edith. And Dulcie was so constituted that she could ask neither of them a favour to save her life.

Lady Conroy then... But how awkward, how disagreeable, how painful to her pride when she had been there only a week and Lady Conroy treated her almost like a sister!... There was a knock at the door.

"Come in!" said Dulcie, surprised. No-one ever came to her little sitting-room at this hour, about half-past five. Who could it be? To her utter astonishment and confusion the servant announced Mr. Valdez.

DULCIE WAS SITTING ON THE sofa, still in her hat and coat, her eyes red with crying, for she had utterly given way when she got home. She was amazed and confused at seeing the composer, who came calmly in, holding a piece of music in his hand.

"Good morning, Miss Clay. Please forgive me. I hope I'm not troubling you? They told me Lady Conroy was out but that you were at home and up here; and I hoped—" He glanced at the highly decorated little piano. This room had been known as the music-room before it was given to Dulcie.

"Oh, not at all," she said in confusion, looking up and regretting her crimson and swollen eyes and generally unprepared appearance.

He immediately came close to her, sat down on a chair opposite her sofa, leant forward and said abruptly, in a tone of warm sympathy:

"You are distressed. What is it, my child? I came up to ask you to play over this song. But I shall certainly not go now till you've told me what's the matter."

"Oh, I can't," said Dulcie, breaking down.

He insisted:

"You can. You shall. I'm sure I can help you. Go on."

Whether it was his personality which always had a magnetism for her, or the reaction of the shock she had had, Dulcie actually told him every word, wondering at herself. He listened, and then said cooly:

"My dear child, you're making a mountain out of a molehill. People mustn't worry about trifles. Just before the war I won a lot of money at Monte Carlo. I simply don't know what to do with it. Stop!" he said, as she began to speak. "You want a hundred and ten pounds. You shall have it in half-an-hour. I shall go straight back to Claridge's in a taxi, write a cheque, get it changed—for you won't know what to do with a cheque, or at any rate it would give you more trouble—and send you the money straight back by my servant or my secretary in a taxi." He stood up. "Not another word, my dear Miss Clay. Don't attach so much importance to money. It would be a bore for you to have to bother Lady Conroy. I understand. Don't imagine you're under any obligation; you can pay it me back just whenever you like and I shall give it to the War Emergency Concerts. . . Now, *please*, don't be grateful. Aren't we friends?"

"You're too kind," she answered.

He hurried to the door.

"When my secretary comes back she will ask to see you. If anyone knows you have a visitor say I sent you the music or tickets for the concert. Good-bye. Cheer up now!"

In an hour from the time Valdez had come in to see her, father and stepmother had each received the money. The situation was saved.

DULCIE MARVELLED AT THE ACTION and the manner in which it was done. But none who knew Valdez well would have been in the least surprised. He was the most generous of men, and particularly he could not bear to see a pretty girl in sincere distress through no fault of her own. It was Dulcie's simple sincerity that pleased him. He came across very little of it in his own world. That world was brilliant, distinguished, sometimes artistic, sometimes merely *mondain*. But it was seldom sincere. He liked that quality best of all. He certainly was gifted with it himself.

FROM THIS TIME, THOUGH VALDEZ still encouraged Dulcie to sing and occasionally accompanied her, the slight tinge of flirtation vanished from his manner. She felt he was only a friend. Did she ever regret it? Perhaps, a little.

XXIX

B ruce, said Edith, "I've just had a letter from Aylmer, from Eastcliff."
"Oh yes," said Bruce. "Got him off to the seaside at last, did
they?"

It was a Sunday afternoon. Bruce was sitting in a melancholy
attitude on a sofa in Edith's boudoir; he held *The Weekly Dispatch* in his
hand, and was shaking his head over a pessimistic article when his wife
came in.

Bruce was always depressed now, and if he felt a little more cheerful
for a moment he seemed to try and conceal it. No doubt his melancholy
was real enough, but it was also partly a pose and a profession. Having
undertaken to be depressed, he seemed to think it wrong to show a
gleam of brightness. Besides, on Sundays Madame Frabelle usually
listened to him; and this afternoon she had gone, unaccompanied, to
hear the Rev. Byrne Fraser preach. Bruce felt injured.

He had grown to feel quite lost without her.

"He's very dull there," said Edith.

"I dare say he is," he answered. "I'm sure *I* should feel half inclined
to cut my throat if I were alone, with a game leg, at a place like that.
Besides, they've had the Zepps there already once. Just the place for
them to come again."

"He's very bored. But he's much better, and he's going back to the
front in a fortnight."

"In a fortnight! Good heavens! Pretty sharp work."

"It is, indeed. He's counting the hours till he can get off."

Bruce, sighing, lighted his cigarette.

"I wondered if you'd mind, Bruce, if I went down for the day to see
him?"

"Mind! Oh *dear*, no! Of course, go. I think it's your duty, poor old
chap. I wondered you didn't run down for the weekend."

"I didn't like to do that," she said.

"Why on earth not?" said Bruce. "Hard luck for a poor chap with
no-one to speak to. Going back again; so soon too."

"Well, if you don't mind I *might* go down tomorrow for a couple of
days, and take Dilly."

"Do," said Bruce eagerly; "do the kid good."

Edith looked at him closely.

"Wouldn't you miss her, now that Archie's at school too? Wouldn't the house seem very quiet?"

"Not a bit!" exclaimed Bruce with emphatic sincerity. "Not the least bit in the world! At least, of course, the house *would* seem quiet, but that's just what I like. I *long* for quiet—yearn for it. You don't half understand my condition of health, Edith. The quieter I am, the less worried, the better. Of course, take Dilly. *Rather*! I'd *like* you to go!"

"All right. I'll go tomorrow morning till Tuesday or Wednesday. But wouldn't it seem the least bit rude to Madame Frabelle? She talks of going away soon, you know."

"Oh, she won't mind," said Bruce decidedly. "I shouldn't bother about her. We never treat her with ceremony."

WHEN, A LITTLE BIT LATER, Madame Frabelle came in (with a slight perfume of incense about her, and very full of a splendidly depressing sermon she had heard), she heartily agreed with Bruce. They both persuaded Edith to run down on the Monday and stay till Wednesday evening at least.

"Perhaps we shall never meet again," said Bruce pleasantly, as Edith, Dilly and the nurse were starting; "either the Zeppelins may come while you're away, or they may set your hotel at Eastcliff on fire. Just the place for them."

"Well, if you want me you've only to telephone, and I can be back in a little more than an hour."

Madame Frabelle accompanied Edith to the station. She said to her on the way:

"Do you know, Edith, I'm half expecting a telegram which may take me away. I have a relative who is anxious for me to go and stay with her, an aunt. But even if I did go, perhaps you'd let me come back to you after?"

Edith assented. Somehow she did not much believe either in the telegram nor the relative. She thought that her friend talked like that so as to give the impression that she was not a fixture; that she was much sought after and had many friends, one or two of whom might insist on her leaving the Ottleys soon.

Aylmer was at the little Eastcliff station to meet them. Except that he walked with the help of a stick, he seemed well, and having put Dilly, the nurse and the luggage in a cab, he proposed to Edith to walk to the hotel.

"This *was* angelic of you, Edith. How jolly the child looks!—like a live doll."

"You didn't mind my bringing her?"

"Why, I'm devoted to her. But, you know, I hope it wasn't done for any conventional reasons. Headley and I are in the Annexe, nearly half-a-mile from you."

"I know," said Edith.

"And when you see the people here, my dear, nobody on earth that counts or matters!—people whom you've never seen before and never will again. But I've been counting the minutes till you came. It really isn't a bad little hole."

He took her down to a winding path covered in under trees, which led to the sea by steps cut in the rock. They sat down on a bench. The sea air was fresh and soothing.

"This is where I sit and read—and think about you. Well, Edith, are you going to put me out of my suspense? How much longer am I to suffer? Let me look at you."

She looked up at him. He smiled at what he saw.

"It'll be rather jolly to have two days or so here all to ourselves," he said, "but it will be far from jolly unless you give me that promise."

"But doesn't the promise refer to after you come back again?" she said in a low voice.

"I don't ask you to come away until I'm back again. But I want you to promise before that you will."

Nothing more was said on the subject at the time, but after dinner, when Dilly had been put to bed, it was so warm that they could come out again, and then she said:

"Aylmer, don't worry yourself any more. I mean to do it."

"You do!"

He looked at her ecstatically.

"Oh, Edith! I'm too happy! Do you quite realise, dear, what it is? . . . I've been waiting for you for four years. Ever since that night I met you at the Mitchells'. Do you know that before the war, when I came into that money, I was wild with rage. It seemed so wasted on me. I had no use for it then. And when I first met you I used to long for it. I hated being hard up. . . The first time I had a gleam of hope was when they told me I'd got over the operation all right. I couldn't believe my life would be spared, for nothing. And now—you won't change your mind again?"

Edith convinced him that she would not. They sat hand in hand, perhaps as near perfect happiness as two human beings can be. . .

"We shall never be happier than we are now," said Edith in a low voice.

"Oh, shan't we?" he said. "Rubbish! Rot! What about our life when I come back again?—every dream realised!"

"And yet your going to risk it," said Edith.

"Naturally; that's nothing. I shall come back like a bad penny, don't you worry. Edith, say you mean it, *again*."

"Say I mean what?"

"Say you love me, you'll marry me. You and the children will belong to me. You won't have any regrets? Swear you won't have any regrets and remorse!"

"I never will. You know, Aylmer, I am like that. Most women know what they want till they've got it, and then they want something else! But when I get what I want I don't regret it."

"I know, my darling sensible angel! . . . Edith, to think this might have happened three years ago!"

"But then I *would* have had regrets."

"You only thought so," he answered. "I should have made you forget them very soon! Don't you feel, my dear, that we're made for each other? I know it."

"Aylmer, how shall I be able to bear your going out again? It will be like a horrible nightmare. And perhaps all we've both gone through may be for nothing!"

"No, now I've got your promise everything will be all right. . . I feel I shall come back all right. . . Look here, darling, you need not be unhappy with Bruce. We're not going to deceive him. And when I come back, we'll tell him. Not till then. There is really no need."

They walked together to the Annexe, which was entered by a small flight of stone steps from the garden. Here Aylmer had a little suite of rooms. Edith went into the sitting-room with him and looked round.

"It's ten o'clock and you're here for your health! Call Headley and go to bed, there's a good boy."

He held both her hands.

"I mustn't ask you to stay."

"*Aylmer*! With Dilly here! And Bruce let me come down to look after you! He was quite nice about it."

"All right, dear, all right. . . I know. No. I'm looking forward to when I come back. . . Go, dear, go."

Edith walked very slowly down the steps again. He followed her back into the garden.

"And suppose—you didn't come back," she said in a very low voice.

Aylmer glanced round: there was no-one in the garden.

"I'm on my honour here," he said. "Go, dear, go. Go in to Dilly." He gave her a little push.

"One kiss," said Edith.

He smiled.

"Darling girl, I've told you before that's a thing I can't do. I really oughtn't to be alone with you at all until we're quite free. . ."

"But I feel we're engaged," said Edith simply. "Is it wrong to kiss your fiancée?"

"Engaged? Of course we're engaged. Wrong? Of course it's not wrong! Only. . . I *can't*! Haven't got the self-command. . . I do believe you're made of ice, Edith—I've often thought so."

"Yes," said Edith, "I dare say you're right."

Aylmer laughed.

"Nonsense! Good night, my darling—don't catch cold. And, Edith."

"Yes, Aylmer?"

"I'll meet you here at nine o'clock tomorrow morning."

"Yes, Aylmer."

"Then you'd better go back in the afternoon. It won't do for you to stay another night here. Oh, Edith, how happy we *shall* be!"

He watched her as she walked across the garden and went into the hotel at the front door. Then he went indoors.

THE NEXT DAY EDITH, DILLY and the nurse went back to London early in the afternoon.

XXX

E dith, during the short journey home, sat with a smile on her lips, thinking of a little scene she had seen before leaving Eastcliff from the hall, known as the lounge, of the hotel. She had watched Dilly, beaming with joy, playing with a particularly large air-ball, bright rose colour, that Aylmer had bought her from a well-known character of the place, a very old woman, who made her living by the sale of these old-fashioned balloons. Dilly was enchanted with it. She had said to Aylmer when the old woman passed with a quantity of them. "They look like flowers; they ought to have a pretty scent," which amused him immensely. As she held it in her hand, pressing it with her tiny finger, a tragedy happened. The air-ball burst. Edith could hardly help laughing at seeing Dilly's expression. It was despair—gradual horror—shock, her first disillusion! Then as tears were welling up in the large blue eyes—she was saying: "Oh, it's dead!"—Edith saw Aylmer snatch the collapsed wreck from the child's hand and run as fast as he could (which was not very fast, and only when leaning on a stick) after the old woman. . . He caught her as she turned the corner, brought back a pink and a blue air-ball and gave them to Dilly, one for each hand. The child beamed again, happier than at first, threw her arms round his neck and kissed him. How touched and delighted Edith was! Would Bruce *ever* have done such a thing? Aylmer had so thoroughly appreciated the little drama of joy, disillusion and consolation shown in the expression in Dilly's lovely little face. Had anything been wanting to Edith's resolution this small incident would have decided it.

WHEN THEY ARRIVED HOME, A day sooner than they were expected, the servant told Edith at the door that Madame Frabelle had gone away.

"Gone without seeing me?"

"Yes, madam. A telegram came for her and she left last night. Here is a letter for you, madam."

Edith ran into the dining-room and tore it open.

MY DEAREST EDITH (it said),
"To my great regret a wire I half expected came, and I was compelled to leave before your return, to join my relative, who is ill. I can't tell you how sorry I am not to say good-bye

and thank you for your dear kind hospitality. But I'll write again, a long letter. I hope also to see you later. I will give you my address next time.

"May I say one word? I can't say half enough of my gratitude for your kindness and friendship, but, apart from that, may I mention that I fear your husband *is very unwell indeed*, his nerves are in a terrible state, and I think his condition is more serious than you suppose. He should be humoured in everything, not worried, and allowed to do whatever he likes. Don't oppose any of his wishes, dear. I say this for your and his own good. Don't be angry with him or anybody. Never think me wanting in gratitude and friendship.

> Truly, I am still your affectionate friend,
> EGLANTINE

What a strange letter. How like her to lay down the law about Bruce! It irritated Edith a little, also it made the future seem harder.

About four o'clock Landi called unexpectedly. He always came just when Edith wanted him most, and now she confided in him and told him of her promise to Aylmer.

He approved of their resolution to wait till Aylmer returned from the front and to have nothing on their conscience before. He was indeed much relieved at the postponement.

"And how is the Spanish girl?" he asked. "How does she get on with Lady Conroy?"

"Oh, all right. She's not Spanish at all. She had rather a blow last week, poor girl. Her father nearly went bankrupt; she was quite in despair. It seems your friend Valdez came to the rescue in the most generous way, and she's immensely grateful."

"He helped her, did he?" said Landi, smiling.

"He seems to have behaved most generously and charmingly. Do you think he is in love with her, Landi?"

"Very likely he will be now."

"And she—she adores Aylmer. Will she fall in love with Valdez out of gratitude?"

"C'est probable. C'est à espérer. . . Enfin-mais toi, mon enfant?"

"And where is Madame Frabelle?" asked Landi.

Edith looked at the postmark.

"Apparently she's at Liverpool, of all places; but she may be going somewhere else. I haven't got her address. She says she'll write."

"C'est ça. . . When does Aylmer return to the front?"

"He goes before the Board tomorrow and will know then."

That evening, when Bruce came in, Edith was struck by his paleness and depression; and she began to think Madame Frabelle was right; he must be really ill. Then, if he was, could she, later, be so cruel as to leave him? She was in doubt again. . .

"Very bad news in the evening papers," he said.

"Is it so bad?"

"Edith," said Bruce, rather solemnly, without listening, "I want to speak to you after dinner. I have something serious to say to you".

"Really?"

"Yes, really."

Edith wondered. Could Bruce suspect anything? But apparently he didn't, since he spoke in a very friendly way of Aylmer, saying that he hoped he wouldn't stop away long. . .

The dinner passed in trivial conversation. She described Eastcliff, the hotel, the people. Bruce appeared absent-minded. After dinner she went to join him in the library, where he was smoking, and said:

"Well, Bruce, what is it you have to say to me?"

"Good heavens," said Bruce, looking at his writing-desk, "if I've spoken of this once I've spoken of it forty times! The inkstand is too full!"

"Oh! I'm so dreadfully sorry," said Edith, feeling the strangeness of Bruce's want of sense of proportion. He had, as it seemed, to speak to her about some important matter. Yet the inkstand being too full attracted his attention, roused his anger! She remembered he had said these very words the day he came back from his elopement with the art student.

Edith looked round the room, while Bruce smoked. And so she had really made up her mind! She *meant* to leave him! Not that she intended to see Aylmer again now, except once, perhaps, to say good-bye.

But still, she really intended to change her whole life when he returned again. She felt rather conscience-stricken, but was glad when she looked at Bruce that there had never been anything as yet but Platonic affection between her and Aylmer, which she could have no cause to blush for before Bruce. And how grateful she felt to Aylmer for his wonderful self-control. Thanks to that, she could look Bruce in the face. . . Bruce was speaking.

"Edith," he said with some agitation, "I wish to tell you something."

She saw he looked pale and nervous.

"What is it, Bruce?" she asked kindly.

"It's this," he said in a somewhat pompous tone, "I am in a very strange condition of health. I find I can no longer endure to live in London; I must get away from the war. The doctor says so. If I'm to keep sane, if I'm not to commit suicide, I must give up this domestic life." She stared at him. "Yes, I'm sorry, I've tried to endure it," he went on. "I can't stand the responsibility, the anxiety of the children and everything. I'm—I'm going away."

She said nothing, looking at him in silence.

"Yes. I'm going to America. I've taken my passage. I'm going on Friday. . . I thought of leaving without telling you, but I decided it was better to be open."

"But, Bruce, do you mean for a trip?"

He stood up and looked at her full in the face.

"No, I don't mean for a trip. I want to live in America."

"And you don't want me to come too?"

"No, Edith; I can't endure married life any longer. It doesn't suit me. Three years ago I offered you your freedom and you refused to take it; I offer it you again now. You are older, you are perfectly fit to manage your life and the children's without me. I must be free—free to look after my health and to get away from everything!"

"You mean to leave us altogether then?" said Edith, feeling unspeakably thankful.

"Exactly. That's just what I do mean."

"But will you be happy—comfortable—alone in America?"

He walked across the room and came back.

"Edith, I'm sorry to pain you, but I shall not be alone."

Edith started, thinking of Madame Frabelle's letter. . . from Liverpool! Evidently they were going away together.

"Of course I give up the Foreign Office and my salary there, but you have some money of your own, Edith; it will be enough for you and the children to live quietly. And perhaps I shall be able to afford to send you part of my income that my father left me when I get something to do over there," he added rather lamely.

"You mean to get something to do?"

"Yes; when I'm strong enough. I'm very ill—very."

There was a long pause, then Edith said kindly:

"Have you any fault to find with me, Bruce?"

"Edith, you are a perfect mother," he said in a peculiar tone which sounded to Edith like an echo of Madame Frabelle. "I've no fault to find with you either as a wife. But I'm not happy here. I'm miserable. I implore you not to make a scene. Don't oppose me; forgive me—on account of my health. This will save my life."

If he only knew how little she wished to oppose him! She stood up.

"Bruce, you shall do exactly as you like!"

He looked enchanted, relieved.

"I hope you will be happy and well, and I shall try to be. May I just ask—is Madame Frabelle going to America?"

"Edith, I will not deny it. We mean to throw in our lot together! Look out! You'll have the inkstand over!" She had moved near the writing-table.

Edith stopped herself from a hysterical laugh.

"You won't mind if I go down to the club for an hour?"

"Certainly not."

"And, Edith—say what you can to my mother, and comfort her. Tell her it's to save my going off my head, or committing suicide. Will you say that?"

"I will," she replied.

Five minutes later the door banged. Bruce had gone to the club. He hadn't told her he had taken a room there, and the same evening he sent up for his luggage. He did not wish to see Edith again.

Just before he went out, as if casually for an hour at the club, Edith had said:

"Would you like to come and see Dilly asleep?"

It had occurred to her that at least he had been frank and honest, and for that he deserved to see Dilly again.

"Edith, my nerves won't stand scenes. I'd better not. I won't see her."

"Oh, very well!" she cried indignantly. "I offered it for your sake. I would rather you *didn't* see her."

"Try not to be angry, Edith. Perhaps—some day—"

"No. Never."

"You would never let me come back again to see you all?"

"Never. Never."

"Edith."

"Yes."

"Oh! nothing. You needn't be so cross. Remember my health."

"I do," said Edith.

"And—Edith."

"Yes, Bruce?"

"Don't forget about that inkstand, will you? It's always filled just a little too full. It's—it's very awkward. . . Remember about it, won't you?"

"Yes. Good night."

"Good night."

And Bruce went to the club.

THE NEXT DAY EDITH FELT she could neither write nor telephone to Aylmer. Just once—only once, for a long time—she must see him.

She confided in Landi, who invited them both to tea at his studio for once only and was urgent in impressing patience on them.

WHEN EDITH ARRIVED WITH THIS thrilling piece of news to announce she found Aylmer alone in the pretty white studio. Landi was expected back every moment from a lesson at a pupil's house.

AYLMER WAS BEAMING WITH JOY. "Oh, my dear!" he cried, "I'm not going away at all! They won't have me! They've given me an appointment at the War Office."

"Oh, Aylmer! How wonderful! I know now—I couldn't have borne your going out again—now."

He put his arm round her. Ah! this, she felt, was real love—it wrapped her round, it lifted her off her feet.

"But now, Aylmer, we mustn't meet, for a long time."

"But, why not? What is it? Something has happened!"

"Aylmer, I needn't keep my promise now."

"What do you mean?"

"Aylmer, Bruce wants to leave me. He's going to leave me—to desert me. And the children, too."

"What! Do you mean—Do you mean—like before?"

"Yes. But this time he won't come back. And he wants me to divorce him. And—this time—I shall!"

"Edith! And do you mean—will he want to marry again?"

"Yes, of course! And she'll take care of him—he'll be all right."

"Oh, Edith!" exclaimed Aylmer. "Thank heaven for Madame Frabelle!"

A Note About the Author

Ada Leverson (1862–1933) was a British novelist. Born into a middle-class Jewish family, Leverson was raised alongside eight siblings by Samuel Henry Beddington, a wool merchant, and his wife Zillah. At 19, she married Ernest Leverson, with whom she would raise a daughter, Violet. In the 1890s, she embarked on a career as a professional writer, submitting stories and articles to *Punch*, *The Yellow Book*, and *The Saturday Review*. Through her work as a theater critic, she gained a reputation for her abundant wit and satirical tone, parodying friends and enemies alike in some of England's most popular magazines and newspapers. She was a devoted friend of Oscar Wilde, who supported her literary pursuits and shared her humorous outlook on life. When Wilde was put on trial for his homosexuality, Leverson offered him a place to stay and continued corresponding with the Irish author until the end of his life. She wrote several novels throughout her life, including *The Twelfth Hour* (1907) and *Little Ottleys* (1908–1916), a trilogy inspired by her troubled marriage to Ernest, who abandoned her in 1905 to move to Canada. Although far from a bestselling author in her time, Leverson has come to be seen as a pioneering artist whose works display a keen understanding of society's triumphs and shortcomings.

A Note from the Publisher

Spanning many genres, from non-fiction essays to literature classics to children's books and lyric poetry, Mint Edition books showcase the master works of our time in a modern new package. The text is freshly typeset, is clean and easy to read, and features a new note about the author in each volume. Many books also include exclusive new introductory material. Every book boasts a striking new cover, which makes it as appropriate for collecting as it is for gift giving. Mint Edition books are only printed when a reader orders them, so natural resources are not wasted. We're proud that our books are never manufactured in excess and exist only in the exact quantity they need to be read and enjoyed.

bookfinity™

Discover more of your favorite classics with Bookfinity™.

- Track your reading with custom book lists.
- Get great book recommendations for your personalized Reader Type.
- Add reviews for your favorite books.
- AND MUCH MORE!

Visit **bookfinity.com** and take the fun Reader Type quiz to get started.

Enjoy our classic and modern companion pairings!